Praise for *Death and Redemption*

"Margarete Ledwez has once again captured the essence of adventure, history and mystery linking an eclectic group of characters from young lives to lives lost. She skillfully places a unique stamp on each individual, leading the reader to believe that she has had a personal relationship with each of them. Whether you want to peek around the corner and merely watch as they approach danger or you're shouting at them to turn back, you'll want to delve into this third instalment of Margarete's well-crafted novels."

—Barry Wills

DEATH AND REDEMPTION

Niagara Tunnels' Secrets Unraveled

The Final Chapter of the Niagara Tunnels Mystery

Margarete Ledwez

ISBN 978-1-943492-69-5 (hard back)
ISBN 978-1-943492-70-1 (soft cover)

Front and back cover photographs © 2019 by Shawn Ledwez

Book and cover design by **designpanache**.

To three very special members of my family. Established over 50 years ago, we continue to enjoy our children and grandchildren. "They are our richest blessings." My children have given us an abundance of joy, topping it off with the extension of themselves and us in the form of grandchildren. I have dedicated earlier books to some already, and want to dedicate this third book to a special three who have blessed us and persevered beyond measure.

Our first born Joel has given so much from the time he was born and has become a handsome young man. I honour his dedication to loving people for who they are; his compassion to love and look beyond what you see. I love his deep thinking spirit, and hugs that say, "I am with you right now." Thank you for inspiring my life for many years.

Lauren, our second born grandchild, has had Hutzpah since day one. Creative as well as beautiful, she has overcome obstacles in her life that none of us thought we would ever have to face. She has overcome these and we are so proud of her and her life. It is so wonderful to watch her live life with love.

Adam is our 7th and youngest grandchild. What a delight he is! He loves creating, especially woodwork and art. He is a wonderful musician. We are so proud of how Adam has overcome so many obstacles in his young life. He is an inspiration, showing us that even if life is not always fair, it can turn around, and good things can happen.

Each of them has been tried and tested in various ways and come through the fire with dignity and love in their hearts. May this dedication be praise for their success.

Contents

Characters

Josh—*main character*

Pa—*Josh's grandfather*

Dad—*Josh's dad Shawn*

Nerissa—*Josh's mom*

Bee—*Josh's sister*

Kelvin—*from Lancaster*

Grammy—*Nerissa's mother*

Grammpy—*Nerissa's father*

Omz—*Shawn's mother*

Mark—*Josh's friend*

Mac—*Josh's friend*

Fritz—*descendant of Friezen*

Stephan—*the father of Fritz*

Mel—*Gondolier*

Andy—*Intruder*

Bella—*Andy's sister*

Barry—*Mac's dad*

Vanessa—*Mac's mom*

Girl—*cougar*

Sweetheart—*cougar*

Halfpint—*cougar*

Dustin—*German friend*

Mitchell—*Dustin's brother*

Mary—*descendant of Mr. Schwartz*

Carly—*Bee's friend*

Rachel—*Bee's friend*

Chelbee—*Rachel's sister*

Angela—*Mark's mom*

Eckert Kempt—*prisoner*

Rudy Kempt—*prisoner*

Herman Wolfgang—*soldier*

Lola—*Lauren*

Manny—*a teen Josh met in Rio*

Adam—*younger brother of Manny*

Joel—*Manny's brother*

Joseph—*Schultz prisoner*

Jervaih—*squatter*

Lovlyn—*Jervaih's wife*

Clara—*Lovlyn's child*

Antonie Wittfoot—*Pa's mother*

Carmela Pilzer—*descendant of Fry*

Hannah—*Carmela's daughter*

Mr. Eisenhouwer—*Jewish father*

Ramona—*Mr. Eisenhouwer's wife*

Natasha—*Ramona's child*

The Old Map

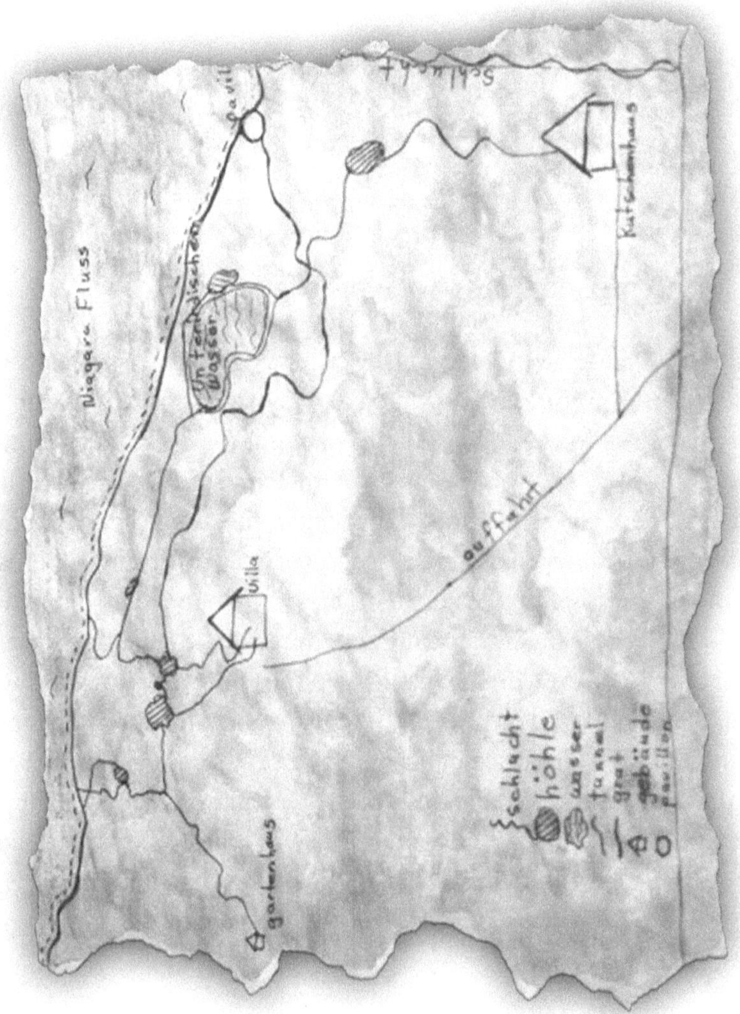

Preface to Book 3

Here we are at the end of our trilogy of stories, and the series of adventures preordained by fate so many years ago. Josh, Mac and everyone close to them continue to hang on for dear life as circumstances unravel, exposing more than their imaginations could have ever dreamed, enduring more danger than most teens could handle. Willing to die rather than see the secrets of Niagara's tunnels exposed, but afraid that there might be another Vinnie out there somewhere, the family is cautious in its continued quest for the truth. Traveling to places they never dreamed they would see, never knowing what is lying around the next corner, the tunnels become a refuge for our intrepid heroes. They are determined to bring the past in line with the present, so that the atrocities of the past may become the family's strength for the future. In this conclusion, South America beckons, but death is never further away than the nearest gang member.

CHAPTER 1

What Next

Another school year was almost over and we still had so much to do. It would soon be two years since I had discovered the tunnels under the old mansion. We felt like it was all just taking too long. The tunnel excursion to the hydro plant had not taken place yet, as Dad and Pa were busy with the new addition. Dad was getting tired of all the planning and town meetings regarding our new build. It was a historic old house and every committee wanted to put stipulations and guidelines on the remodel. It was tiring to say the least. We were no closer to ending the search for ancestors than last summer, as no one could get away for a few weeks at a time. It left us extremely grateful for the ancestors Mom and Dad found in Germany and Italy last year. It was comforting to know, they were good people just like those forefathers, which died for noble causes during the war. The gold we found would make a huge difference to the remaining relatives. Of course, only once we were free to share the truth with them.

Bee was threatening to run away and get married, although I knew she was just kidding. She missed Kelly as much as he missed her. She had graduated this past spring and worked hard on her studies. She wasn't sure if she would take some extra courses or start to work full time.

Grammy and Grammpy had been ready to move since last year, leaving only their necessities unpacked. They were also tired of the wait. Mom kept encouraging them to move in with us, but they would not hear of it. They were fortunate to stay in their home until the addition was completed. The buyer of their farm was going to demolish the old home when it was vacant, as he was building on the far side of the acreage. They would not interfere with the buyer taking ownership and could remain living there until the annex to our house was finished. After all, they didn't use hydro, gas or city water. They would incur no expense to the new owners. We took solace in the fact that the gold was safely stored and hidden away. The maps and other documents, as well as the wills the prisoners left behind, were beside the gold in our gigantic safe. Who would have thought that these ancestors would have a chance to write out wills and leave their story and money to those who were now living? The safe was out of sight in the old mansion and we felt confident that we had made the right choice, to hide it there. We hoped Barry would not get more suspicious and be driven to find our secret entrances to the tunnels below.

We regularly took snacks down for Girl and Sweetheart, and they came to meet us often. The townspeople were still paranoid, as the cougars had been spotted more often than in the past months.

The soldiers' families were researched and we found some had moved to South America after the war. Hopefully, they stayed in one area so they would be easy to locate. Pa would continue to do his magic and find the ancestors.

Pa, Dad and I gathered as many supplies as we could and placed them in passages below. The next trip into the tunnels would be a longer one, and it might take days. We put some of our supplies in the large lake tunnel. That seemed the most likely place to start looking. I knew of one tunnel that we had not explored yet. That one was down where we found the pile of bones. It was a place we did not want to disturb if at all possible. We considered it a tomb-like grave site. We would reverently have a look around, but only after Grammy and Grammpy were moved in. We were sure we had found all the gold. There were twelve gold bars and twelve portions of coins. Pa figured the remaining ancestors would receive well over $1,000,000.00 per family. We had big plans for these people, revealing much and hoped we could execute our plan without a glitch.

Deep underground, in the cavern containing the bones, we were delivering some supplies and had a quick look around. The work to move supplies to the bottom was a grueling feat. Our leg muscles burned and my arms felt like they were going to fall off. It was a long way down the stone stairs, even without carrying the extra weight. We needed to rest. The lanterns were lit. Our flashlights illuminated the pile of bones still clad in rags. We were looking to see if it would be possible to separate the remains of the prisoners when I noticed an odd skeletal hand.

"Look! Look! It is Friedrich's hand."

Dad and Pa hurried over to look down and see the skeleton with the missing fingers. Pa was shocked, although he suspected his uncle would be among the dead. It was difficult to realize the inhumane death that befell these men, not to mention the terrible existence they endured building the tunnels. They were prisoners, there against their wills and died here. He knelt down and took a close look at the hand with the missing fingers. It was isolated and had been stretched out away from the skeletal remains. His body was on the bottom. He must have landed on the cold rock surface, being one of the first to fall. Pa wanted so badly to ignore the facts.

He kept repeating, "No ... No ... No ... I have seen the works of your hands, I have read the words they have written; now I see what is left of them. These hands stroked my head, they kissed my forehead, and they picked me up to hug me. It is too much," he cried.

He needed to get it out. I felt compassion as my eyes filled with tears. The reality was that Friedrich was my relative too. These were his bones. To see the actual skeleton of my ancestor brought the reality from my head to my heart. We had to face the horrible truth of his demise. It was Friedrich himself, lying there in skeleton form, dressed in rags! I couldn't handle the thought and how he was forced to fall to his death. Dad, also wiping his tears with the handkerchief he religiously carried, comforted Pa. They stood together for a moment when no words could measure with the thoughts and sadness they felt. Pa hadn't even seen his uncle since he was a young boy but remembered all the great times his uncle had planted in his heart. He made Pa feel so special and spent so much time with him. He was important to his parents and they spoke often of their lost bothers.

They thought and spoke of him and his brother Daniel, for years, not knowing what happened to them. They expected them to show up one day, as many did, very suddenly, after the war. We had to get a grip on ourselves and were spurred on to discover all the secrets we could for our relatives. Dad and Pa took a few moments to reminisce as I listened on, trying to remember every detail. When Pa was ready, we moved on.

The tunnel we needed to explore was directly behind the mound of bones. We would be careful not to disturb what was left of these heroes, until their relatives could pay their last respects to them. The trip into this tunnel would happen another day. Today we had experienced enough, and Pa looked tired. It was a long climb back up the stairs, and we needed to get him back.

CHAPTER 2

It is Finished

After months of grueling work, Pa and Dad finally got the annex to the house built and it was ready for Grammy and Grammpy to move in. The elderly couple were just tying up loose ends in Lancaster, visiting friends and so on. Bee, visiting whenever possible, had been extremely helpful in so many ways. She especially helped in transferring the couple's bank accounts, to the Meridian Bank in Virgil. The town would be a nice place for them to get the banking, groceries and other chores done. Electronics still baffled the elderly couple, and they would not only prefer the personal touch, but insisted on banking by speaking to a teller. Many Amish people did not put a penny of their money in the bank. The hardware stores in Lancaster sold huge safes, almost as big as ours, for this reason. All of Grammy and Grammpy's furniture had been sold except for their favorite chairs and the small side tables, where the Bibles rested when not being read. Even Bee's bedroom at Grammy's had been taken apart. She hated to see it go. Grammy kept her dishes and all the little things needed for everyday living. It wasn't much. They lived a modest lifestyle. Grammy brought her handmade quilts and even gave Bee the one from her bedroom at the farm house. Bee assured Grammy that she would cherish it in the years to come. Kelly did not want to accept any cast offs, as his one room residence couldn't squeeze in another thing.

Of course, it would be difficult to say goodbye, not only to simple possessions, but mostly the people. They had spent most of their lives here, amongst the Amish. It used to be a quiet and tranquil way of life, until the tourists took over the small towns in the area. Grammpy would miss helping the farmers with repairing their tools. He was known by everyone to be able to repair anything. Grammy would miss the relationships with her endless number of friends, who had also become her life.

Bee and Kelly would rent a truck and accompany Grammy and Grammpy back to Niagara, where they would live with the family.

Mom had painted all the rooms white, as that is what her parents were used to. Even the woodwork was white. The floors were done in a rustic wide planked vinyl hardwood look. The warmth would radiate up from the in-floor heating. The open concept residence, drew your eyes into the stylish kitchen, with its sanitized looking Carrera Marble counters and stainless appliances. We were grateful to Kenneth Builders for their patience with the renovation, as everyone's needs had to be met. Grammpy had done his research well in finding this company, talking to many who the builder had gotten good reports from. Radiant Plumbing finishing the job, was the last one on the scene to install the dishwasher and the ice maker in the fridge. Dave the plumber, was kind enough to give the seniors a run down on how to use the ice maker and dishwasher. Grammy had so much to learn in her new home, and we hoped it wouldn't make the transition too difficult. Other than the learning curve, the couple was excited and happy with their new home.

The seniors had made trips back to Niagara, to the new build and to pick out their furniture. It was delivered and put into place. Everyone took special care to leave a space for Grammpy's chair, which sat at an angle in front of the window, so he could see what was happening on the yard and driveway. Grammy just wanted a nice corner near the fireplace, for herself.

From my point of view, this was as good as it gets. I could get a meal and good conversation at any time of the day! Buttons would be sewn on and mending done, as Grammy loved sewing. I wondered if the couple would be told of the tunnels, or even be able to visit them. Pa would have someone to visit with, while I was in school and while Dad was traveling for work. I also wondered how Omz would have liked the house now and how she would like everyone living with her here. Those huge pots of soup she made would come in very handy around here. I wondered what kind of soup Grammy made? Mom continually raved about them, so I would find out.

We had a couple of days before Bee, Kelly and my grandparents would arrive. We couldn't wait! Kelly would drive the vehicle back to the truck rental, in Lancaster, when he returned after making the life changing delivery to Niagara.

Dad and Pa put a secret door from the main house into the addition. It led from the back-hall closet, near the kitchen of the main house, to the inside of the closet, in the mother-in-law suite laundry room. They also put an entrance into the tunnels below, from the new apartment. The new addition would be well suited to the old mansion in style and intrigue. They did this on their own, in secret, without any help except for Mark and myself. Thankfully the foundations of the house did not interfere with the existing tunnels. The structures below the house, remained uncompromised.

We were moving some furniture around in the new rooms, when someone knocked at the front door.

"It looks like you are busy," Barry said as he stepped in. "I wouldn't have bothered you, but this is important."

"That's okay, come on in," said Dad.

Barry looked too serious and we wondered what was going on? He started with, how the case was going, to find Bella. Barry still thought Bella might have been a passenger in Omz's car, the night of the fatal accident. There were no leads yet. The next sentence caught us off guard, as we were in the remodeling mode and not quite with what Barry was saying.

"We will exhume the body within a couple of days and find out just who is really in that grave."

He had the permit in his hand and gave us some papers to read. There would be some things that we needed to know and might have questions about. Dad and Pa knew all this information but it was certainly new to me. It sounded harsh at the time coming from a friend. Barry had to make it clear that there was no other option and it was a professional call. There was no other way to say it.

We were worried about Pa. We couldn't tell Barry about the tunnel experience, and we knew this ordeal would be even harder on the senior member of our family. Dad asked if we could get equipment and do most of the work ourselves. We wanted as little as possible dug up as the tunnels, could be revealed or compromised. Of course, not knowing any of this, Barry okayed our request. Barry said someone from the police service would have to be on watch and he could be the one that oversaw everything, until the coffin was exposed.

"I am sorry to lay this on your family, just when you are so busy," he apologized.

"We understand," Dad said as he patted Barry on the back. "Thank you for taking the time to tell us in person."

As Barry left, Dad and I looked at each other, not saying a word. Our expressions said it all. Was this going to go well? How would Pa handle this? My Grandfather was the first to speak.

"It is good that we can do the work ourselves, as we know where the tunnel entrance is. We can go out to the graveyard and go over our plans to make sure we familiarize ourselves with the exact location to dig."

No one mentioned the fact that Omz might not be there in the grave, and if not, where would she be? There were no leads on Bella or Omz. Of course, to find out Omz was alive, would be a gift from God, but then, where was she?

We knew exactly what we had to do and where we had to dig. The lightest most compact excavator was ordered. It could lift the marble and yet there wouldn't be much damage done. Dad suggested we start tomorrow morning, bright and early. He notified Barry of the plan and Barry said to start and he would be by as soon as possible. The Forensics Unit would also be called after the body was reached. We were all so nervous to find out who was in the grave. Of course, we didn't want it to be Omz. The thought was planted that she could be alive and we needed her to be and then find her.

The next morning, all was cancelled as we had severe thundershower reports for the duration of the week. Barry agreed that it was not an emergency, and we would wait for better weather. It would put us on hold and wondering, but it was all we could do for now.

Nerissa made a warm meal that night as the weather left you with that damp, cold feeling, even though it was late spring. We enjoyed our fellowship and knew Nerissa was going to be happy, not only having her daughter back but her parents too. They would be close by and she would not have to worry about how they were doing. It was going to be different, and we would have to be careful of private conversations. I suggested that once the elderly couple got settled, we should tell them about the tunnels. Dad would consider it, especially remembering that secrets killed Omz, or made her disappear. We would expect the rest of the family early in the morning; they would leave at night to be here first thing in the morning.

CHAPTER 3

New Beginnings

The truck was packed very quickly as the elderly couple's Amish friends came to help them, as well as say good-bye. The many years of companionship and support received and given would be missed by everyone there. Grammy and Grammpy shed tears as they waved from the moving truck. It was bitter sweet, now that Bee would not have a place to stay when visiting Kelly. In time she would figure it out, maybe Rachel's family would let her stay some times. It was a long drive while they anticipated their arrival home. As they turned at the stone pillars, at the end of the driveway, they could see the house, now visible, beckoning them to come home. It looked so massive to Bee. The landscaping was already done and it looked nicely nestled into the unique backdrop. Angela and Mark, waved to welcome them as they drove by the carriage house. It looked like they were coming over to help their new neighbors move in, even though it was raining. Grammy and Grammpy would feel at home with this display of kindness, it was what they were used to.

It was now pouring, but Dad had an idea. The truck could be backed up as close as possible to the garage and unloaded from there. It worked like a charm. The garage was built higher than most, so the truck just made it into the large doorway. No one even got wet!

The truck was full but in reality, it amounted to just a few things. I know we would have had a transport or two to move our possessions.

Mom and Grammy made the beds and put their clothes away.

Once the pin box appeared on the dresser, we knew their job was done. I wondered if Grammy would change over to our styles, using zippers and buttons? Time would tell. It was not a religious practice for her but one she was used to and never changed.

Bee and Angela put the dishes away as well as the cooking pots and all that a kitchen should hold. I noticed a very huge pot! Wow, was this what Grammy made her soup in?

I had to ask, "Grammy do you make soup in this gigantic pot?"

"Oh, no Josh!" she laughed. "This is what we used to heat our water on the wood stove. "The water was used for cooking, baths and dishes. You know, we did not have hot water when your mother was young!"

I couldn't imagine what that would be like. I have always had hot running water, inside toilets, microwaves, TV and more. Then the tunnels came to mind, a favorite place of mine, very primitive, but I enjoyed its comfort. In fact, next to sitting at our kitchen table, it was my most special place to be.

The living room furniture was a modest set and moved around to Grammpy's liking. I wondered how Grammpy got away with saying where the furniture would be placed. Everyone I knew gave that privilege to the lady of the house. I thought guys didn't care about that stuff.

When Grammy came in, she didn't say a word and walked directly over to the couch as Grammpy took his place on the other side of it ready to lift. It was moved a little closer to and centered with the window. I decided that we all know what our jobs are. Once in a while we get confused and cross over, only to be corrected. It keeps everything moving along smoothly. Grammpy's chair was in its place at the window and Grammy's was next to the fireplace. Their Bibles were resting on the small tables beside the chairs. I wondered at what time my grandparents would read their Bibles?

Mac and her Mom came by with some lunch. It was homemade macaroni and cheese. We initiated the place with a nice meal and our first spill. It was Mark who christened the floor with a glass of milk. Better him than me. The ladies all jumped up as if it was a gallon of paint. There again, it was the ladies, not the men who jumped up. That had to be a task in their job description and not ours?

We decided to let the elderly couple have a nap, as they traveled through the night. Bee and Kelly went to their separate rooms too. Mac, Mark and I hung out down below in the underground living room. It was so much fun just chatting and hanging out down there.

CHAPTER 4

Rainy Day Trouble

Mac came up with the idea of assessing the casket area from the tunnel, under the graveyard. Mark and I laughed, as it was a bizarre idea to look below and not from the top. We could have a look at the area if it wasn't too steep and slippery to get to. We grabbed the old jackets that were kept down below and pushed the cabinet aside, as well as loosened the furs. The board was already easily removed and we were off. We took two bright lanterns and each had a flashlight. I was missing my exploration bag. The tunnel was becoming familiar by now and we felt like nothing could hinder our search. When we got to the cross roads where we could see daylight, we could see it was still pouring outside. We had never checked out the opening, where I was almost swept to my death.

"Let's look over the edge," I ordered.

"Do you think it might be too dangerous?" Mac asked.

"Come on, chicken!" Mark added.

It was slippery but we cautiously made our way towards the daylight. Water was dripping in the tunnel because of the rain. We didn't have to go far to get near to the end, where we saw another cave opening in the rock tunnel.

"Let's check it out!"

"I thought we were going the other way?" Mac protested.

"You know we don't pass up a cave when we find one," Mark retorted.

"I would like to see how far down we are on the gorge," I added.

Mac followed quietly, still not sure that we should be doing this. I gave Mark a boost up into the cave and handed him a lantern. It illuminated the cave beautifully. He loved the coziness of it and noticed the darkness reached further than the light shone.

"Come on in guys, this is great," he pleaded as I gave Mac a push.

It was my turn. I jumped up to hoist myself, and my fingers slipped. My body bounced backwards and towards the edge of the opening. I tried to stop myself but I was out of control and now on my back. I hit my head on the side of the tunnel and went over the edge, still trying to stop. I could watch myself in slow motion, in horror and helplessness.

I heard Mac scream. Later Mark told me the details. He jumped down from his perch, almost out of control like I was. I was out of sight as Mark scanned the gorge for a sight of me.

Mark cried out, "Josh, where are you? Josh!" forgetting about the noise traveling far along the gorge.

Mac ended up on her knees beside him, "Where is he?" She cried.

She sat there and sobbed, knowing her friend was gone. Mark was stunned, as if in a trance. He was in shock. Mac suggested they get help.

She sobbed, "Do you think he is dead?"

There was no response from Mark.

"What do I do? What do I do?" she asked herself.

"Get it together Mac, you can do this," she coached herself.

She led Mark back into the tunnel and sat him down where he would be safe. He had no response and she knew she couldn't trust him at the entrance. When she got him settled, she went back to have another look over the edge. She gently called to see if Josh would answer.

"Josh, answer me please!" she cried. "Where are you?" She pleaded.

It was a desperate time for desperate measures. Mac clung onto a rock with one hand. The rock jutted out at the tunnel entrance and she could lean stretching her body out as far as possible without falling. She scanned slowly and carefully noticing everything that her eyes could take in. There, way down below, she saw Josh's baseball cap. He couldn't have survived that fall. He must be dead. She kept looking to see if she could spot his lifeless body.

"Oh, what should I do? God, show me what to do?" she prayed.

Her eyes started to look closer to where she thought I was.

There were very small layers of rock as you looked down. Could she climb them? She wondered if that would work, as she was willing to try anything. She couldn't leave Mark like this. She didn't know what he would do in his state. She turned to have a look at him. He was gone!

She called, "Mark. Mark where are you?"

No one answered. His flashlight was still lying there but the lantern was gone. There was no light in the back of the tunnel. Was he in the cave again? Why didn't she hear him? She was preoccupied of course, focused on finding Josh. Mac saw a shoe sticking out of the cave entrance! Was Mark lying up there? With difficulty she climbed up to look and found only a shoe. Where was he? She held her lantern high so she could have a good look around. There was another tunnel in the back of this cave and she would enter it. This had to be where Mark went. Taking the flashlight and lantern, she moved carefully to the tunnel and searched its irregular walls. It widened and narrowed. There were carved steps in some areas and others she had to navigate carefully, as the floor grade was quite steep in a downward direction. This was taking too long. If Josh was hurt he needed medical attention, he could die. The thought, of his death was just too much to consider right now and her mind rejected the thought. She needed to get to the bottom to see if she could find Josh. By now, she was hyperventilating and felt like she was going to burst. She started to pray and asked God once again, to help her. She wondered if God helped, when people got themselves into trouble and didn't listen to Him in the first place. She would find out. Mac could feel a draft. She was getting to an opening as she saw a glimmer of light. She was almost there! Would she see Josh smashed on the rocks? Would Mark be there, still in his trance?

The daylight was blinding, even though it was still raining. How long did this take her? She moved out slowly. She saw Josh's hat and carefully moved towards it. The ground seemed solid. She was on a ridge, but nowhere near the bottom. Retrieving the cap, she clutched it close to her, as tears welled up in her eyes. She wiped the blinding blur, as she was trying to look around. Her eyes were straining, but she thought she saw something move above her.

Mac called out with a cracking voice, "Mark is that you?"

"Mark where are you?" she cried out.

"It's me," said a faint voice she should have recognized.

"Who are you?" she pleaded.

"Josh," as he mustered up energy to say his name.

She screamed, "You are alive! You are alive! Thank you, God. Thank you!

"I will be right up, Josh, just stay there. Please don't move."

She looked to see how high he was and wondered if she could climb up to him. It looked treacherous, especially in the rain. Could she reach him from the tunnel above? If there was no other solution, she would have to call for an emergency crew. It would probably expose their secret. Josh's life and Mark's, wherever he was, were more important. She could not imagine life without her two best friends. She started on her way up the tunnel and was going to look at Josh's position in the gorge from the top. It was a hard climb, as she hurried as much as possible, still carrying her lantern and flashlight. She came to the other very small cave entrance. She wondered if it could lead to the outside. Her flashlight revealed a long narrow tunnel that she would have to crawl through. Mac left the lantern and took her flashlight. She crawled in head first, sliding the flashlight ahead of her. It felt like a day went by and her knees were worn raw. Her mother was going to explode when she saw the jeans. Mac knew she could still wear them, with the styles being so primitive these days. It felt like her knees were bleeding and her back was killing her from the tension. There was hope and new enthusiasm when she saw daylight ahead. When she reached the end of the tunnel, she got a full view of... Mark!?

"What are you doing here and why didn't you answer when I called you?" she demanded. "How did you get here?"

"If you would give me a chance to talk, I will tell you," he spoke looking down at his feet, just realizing he was wearing one shoe.

"Oh Josh, how are you?" She exclaimed, trying to see past Mark, to get a look at her other friend.

"Well if you two would stop and check me out, I would be glad to get out of here," he muttered.

Mark told Mac he came to his senses when she screamed, "God show me what to do!" Mac of course protested that she was not screaming. Mark felt compelled to search the cave again and found the small tunnel. He crawled through it to find Josh. He froze in the tunnel at one point and couldn't move. He remembered the last time Josh crawled into the tunnel and helped him. He imagined Josh right in front of him coaxing him, to follow and he moved ahead slowly. Mac was glad he was fine and that he made it through his emotional freeze. Josh seemed to be attentive and could answer all their questions. His eyes looked alert. He said he grabbed whatever he could on the way down. At times the shrubs almost stopped him, but then were ripped out of the ground or slipped out of his hand. He felt if it hadn't been raining, he could have grabbed one and it would have held him.

"But then, who knew what level you would have landed on?" Mac said. "I think this was where you were supposed to land, God's grace." She added, "I know that!"

"Why didn't you answer when I called you, Josh?" she asked.

"I don't know, but I think I was out for a while. I don't know, I didn't hear you." Josh answered.

"It doesn't matter; you are here now." Mac smiled from ear to ear.

Mark helped Josh sit up slowly to see if anything was broken or cut. So far he checked out fine. After a few minutes they helped him stand. He felt pain in his ankle and couldn't step on it. He sat down and they had a close look at it.

"I think it might be broken!" Mark spoke while helping his friend.

Mac examining his foot exclaimed, "It does look swollen and bruised. Your toes are still pointing in the right direction."

"Oh, thanks for the kind words." I retorted.

Mark interrupted, "Okay, I think you are just fine and ready to go, Josh. Mac, you go first, then Josh and I will follow."

Mac wanted to know if Mark would panic. Mark figured he was following Josh, so he should be okay.

It was a tedious job crawling back. Josh did just fine holding his ankle off the ground as he moved. Mark followed along like a trooper. Mac saw the light of the lantern she had left behind. It felt good to stand up. The problem was going to be for Josh to walk. Mark would have to support him. We expressed the devastation we felt when Josh had fallen over the edge not to be seen. Mac talked about her total loss of knowing what to do. Then she saw Mark's shoe.

"Did you put your shoe there?" she asked.

He replied, "No, I didn't even know it was gone until much later!"

Josh said, "Cool!"

Mac reported the double whammy of losing Mark and how it prompted her to action in her search of the cave and tunnel.

Josh confidently spoke when he acknowledged the fact that God had spared his life, even when he knew he should not be in the tunnels. They all agreed that every step could be attributed to God's leading. This was so cool, and the knowledge gave them a great sense of peace within. To be on God's radar was so awesome. Josh was having trouble navigating the smooth steep incline, even with the support. He decided to crawl up those areas, as it eased the pressure on his ankle, and he didn't slide as much. We finally made it back to the underground living room. Josh rested on the cot as Mark and Mac closed the entrance by replacing everything and moving the cabinet back to its rightful place.

Mark and Mac sat on the cot beside Josh and decided what to tell their parents. Mac thought she would just need to explain her jeans. Mark's were badly torn too, but at least his knees were not bleeding. Mac implied that the jeans had a very artistic modern flare and she could wear them providing she could get the bloodstains out. Or should they start a new fashion trend? What should they say about Josh's leg and his goose egg? The three knew very well, that they would never be able to step foot into the tunnels, without an adult escort, if their parents or anyone found out about their near death excursion. Josh would need to see a doctor, or go to the hospital.

If they were noticed before they changed, they would say they accidently slid down the steep hillside on the other side of the gazebo. Josh thought he sprained his ankle, taking the fall, sliding downwards. They had a hard time getting back up and crawled on their knees, as it was too slippery for any other approach. It sounded good to them.

"Hey, you didn't even thank me for retrieving your favorite, "Radiant Plumbing cap!" Mac stated.

Josh uttered as he tried to get up, "Yes, I am glad you retrieved that for me. It comes with good memories of helping finish Grammy and Grammpy's house."

"Yeah, just look at your sweatshirt and cap, you look like a bill board," Mark retorted.

"You guys are just jealous," was my comeback!

I spent a couple of hours at emergency and was glad to find that I had just badly bruised my ankle. I couldn't believe that a bruise could hurt so much! Mom and Dad, as well as Pa, gave me the old evil eye, letting me know that they didn't believe they were getting all, if any of the story. If they only knew! Grammy and Grammpy came for dinner and I had to relay all the details. Bee was getting very melancholy as Kelly was going to leave the next morning for Lancaster. She had no idea when they would see each other again. She had quit her job because she was away so much and had to find another place to create income now that school was over. What would her schedule be and when would she be able to get off work again? Grammy asked how the quilt looked on her bed?

"It looks like it was made for the room, Grammy. It is very beautiful and will remind me of my room on the farm every time I look at it.

"Dat is gut (Amish for, that is good)," Grammy replied.

Grammpy added, "Grammy would like to make an Amish dinner tomorrow. If that is gut?"

We were all excited and talking at once. The door opened and Barry entered.

"I apologize for the intrusion, but I knocked a long time before entering. I heard lots of commotion, so I knew you were home and didn't hear me."

Dad replied, "Don't worry about it, Barry, come on in and have some dinner with us. We were discussing our Amish dinner planned, for tomorrow night."

Barry took a chair and asked what we were having? Everyone added a dish and it sounded like a smorgasbord.

Mom interjected and said, "Why don't you have Vanessa and Mac join us too. I will also ask Angela and Mark."

It was agreed that we would have a party of sorts. It would be fun. I reminded Grammy that this happens often and when you prepare dinner there should always be extra. I added that I loved the leftovers too.

Barry asked how my ankle was and I tried to look as casual about the question as I could. Mac had texted earlier that she got into the house and changed her clothes before she was noticed. Afterwards she told her parents about my ankle being bruised and sliding down the embankment.

Barry wanted to know why I was there in this weather and terrible rainstorm.

Pa helped me out by cutting in and telling Barry he was in too much of a hurry to see the condition of the gazebo. He asked if we could check out the foundation as he and Grammpy were going to repair it after all these years of deterioration. Barry said it would be an awesome view and wondered why it was never done before. Pa added that he had lost interest, especially after Omz death or disappearance. That brought Barry to a new topic. The exhumation. We will have to do that as soon as the weather clears up.

"It is supposed clear up in the next couple of days. We will let the ground dry up and start first thing next week, if that works for you?" Barry kindly asked.

Dad would order the machinery again and have it here first thing Monday morning. It made us all anxious to know the results.

Barry finished his meal and was on his way.

CHAPTER 5

New Friends in Europe

Dad was taking this evening to touch base with his new friends in Germany and Italy. Apparently Jervaih, Lovlyn and Clara were doing very well. Jervaih's job was bringing in a good income and he was able to make more repairs to the house after the living expenses were paid. Lovlyn was expecting again and feeling very nauseous. She had planted a garden and they could live from their harvest. Lovlyn would can vegetables and fruits as the boss's wife gave her boxes of canning jars. Jervaih's boss gave him some chickens if he would supply him with fresh eggs and a cow for the family's fresh milk and butter. He treated Jervaih with kindness and he liked working for him. He helped Jervaih make a wagon to attach to the back of the motorcycle so he could take his family shopping when needed. Clara was enjoying her new surroundings as well. Pa enjoyed hearing about the people that were living in the old family homestead. He could imagine it full of life again. Mom and Dad's timing was just perfect and it was a blessing being able to share with these people.

Next he called Carmela Pilser (Fry). Dad was to find out that Omie Pilser had passed away. Carmela was so grateful for the visit from Mom and Dad. Her Omie died with a peaceful heart, knowing she had told the truth regarding who Carmela was and how she came to be her granddaughter. Carmela and her granddaughter Hannah, thought they might like to come to Canada sometime in the future. Dad thought that was a great idea and he would be in touch regarding the details.

Next, he called Mitchell and Dustin and their mother. They worked during the day, so he needed to call at just the right time. Mary answered and got caught up before she gave the phone to the boys. They were on speakerphone so everyone could hear. The excitement in their voices was overwhelming and we could picture them around their table in the kitchen. In fact, Dad said he could smell and almost taste, the strudel.

They told Dad about the museum causing quite a raucous in the news. Everyone wondered where the discovery was found. They had left the tunnels, rooms and skeletal remains as they were. The museum had managed to make exact copies of what they found hidden under their home. They were able to confirm this when the family was given access to see it for themselves. They felt so proud of their ancestor, who had the fortitude to stand up for his convictions with such vision for the future, as well as give his life for it. People were flocking to put their names on a list to see the museum's newly found artifacts depicting their exact surroundings where they were found. Of course, it was still a mystery where they came from and the reporters were hounding the museum regarding the details. The boys and their mother did not know how long they could be anonymous, before someone leaked the information to the press. Dustin was going to come to Canada and asked if he could stay at our place. He was going to check Canada out and see if there would be enough employment for the two brothers. I was sure the job opportunities were endless, and we would be happy to host him, Mitchell and Mary.

Dustin informed us that Mitchell would take care of their Mother and the business, and Dustin would be here at the end of the month. He would give us the information of his flights and so on, when he booked.

It was getting late, and I don't know how Dad kept everyone straight. I guess they weren't just names to him but real people with faces, and that made it possible. He took the time to call Stephan and Fritz Friezen too.

Fritz answered, "Hello Canada"?

It was nice to hear how well they were doing! Fritz could already go solo with his gondola and his Dad had a job with an accounting firm in

Venice. They were so happy. Their friend Mel, the gondolier, said they were taking all of his business from him. Fritz laughed at the thought. Mel hired Stephan to work for him in the evenings playing his accordion as it promoted more business. Fritz needed some time off in the evenings, which he spent with Mel's daughter, whom he seemed to have a special interest in. Mel's family embraced them as close friends and introduced them to others in Venice. Stephan had abstained from alcohol and stayed sober. How wonderful it was to hear. It was lovely speaking with them and Dad assured them he would call again in the near future, as he had done regularly in the past.

We all got on Facebook and looked them up again. We needed to familiarize ourselves with each family if we wanted to present the past to them, in a way that was worthy of their ancestors.

Kelly didn't know of the ancestors, but knew of our European friends. He couldn't believe how much we knew of them. In the short time we visited them, we had been injected into their lives in such a substantial way. He would find out one day, as it certainly looked like he was becoming a permanent family member. I wondered what having a brother would be like. I would spend more time with this guy to see if he was worthy of my sister?

The next morning Kelly would be off with the truck, to Lancaster rental and then home. His car was at the rental establishment for an easy switch. We all gave our hugs and said good-bye. It was hard for Grammy and Grammpy as they had nurtured Kelly for a few years and now they had to let go. Bee, of course, tried to hold it together as long as he was there, but fell apart soon after. We gave them time to say good-bye and respected their privacy. What an emotional time for Bee and us, because when one person in the family hurts, we all do, whether we want to or not.

At least she would not be alone this evening. We were having everybody over for dinner. It would keep her mind on food and friends instead of Kelly.

CHAPTER 6

Who is in the Grave?

First thing Monday morning we greeted the driver of the excavator. He seemed like a very obliging fellow and easy to work with. We told him we were trying to prevent the graveyard from being dug up and wanted to keep it localized to one grave-site. He agreed that this was best and he would work at getting that done. First the stone was moved. Family members took turns coming over to see what was happening. Mark and Mac were there to support me and be there for everyone else. The excavator reached the casket and we asked if we could do the rest by hand. The driver went to take his break and we shoveled out the rest of the dirt. The excavation wasn't showing any tunnels and we were immensely relieved. The digger had over dug slightly so it could get a hold of the coffin and lift it up. When his break was over, the driver started to retrieve the coffin. We were ready and everyone was there: Dad, Pa, Grammy, Grammpy, Mom, Bee, Angela and my friends. There was no one missing except Omz. Was she here too?

Vanessa showed up just a minute before Barry. He must have called her. Barry arrived alone and the crew he ordered came with their separate truck. We noticed Barry kept a pretty tight timeline.

Bee came and stood beside me, "I hope it isn't Omz! I can't imagine how Pa feels."

Bee and I walked over to stand on each side of Pa for support. Pa said, "You know, we might not even find out today if it is Omz. They will have to do tests to find out."

The men got to work preparing the site. They were gowned up and wore masks. Although our property was private, they put up a screen to hide the grave site. They spread a tarp and disinfected the area. The casket was put on the covered ground with the utmost respect.

The two gentlemen, one from the Unit and the other a Cemeteries Officer, seemed to give the orders with the same respect as you felt at a funeral. They worked quietly and it gave us an eerie feeling. The pit of my stomach was flipping. They checked the nameplate on the casket correspondence and compared it to the name on the license. They would also approve a new casket, but we figured it was not necessary as the casket appeared to be in good condition. The casket was opened and Pa stepped forward. He had told us beforehand, that the body might be totally decayed or just partially. Pa said he could identify Omz even if she was just a skeleton. He stepped forward to do something he had never imagined. After all this time he would try to identify the body. Dad stepped up with Pa and stood beside him. Pa thought the body looked in pretty good shape and was recognizable. He knew the person was not there anymore, their spirit was in a much better place. He first saw the wedding band. It belonged to his wife. Then he saw the gold tooth as the lips had deteriorated somewhat. It was the top right-side tooth. She always wanted to have it removed but never got that far. Even Dad could recognize that it was his mother. None of the rest of the family wanted to see Omz this way, but would rather remember her as the vibrant person she was. Since Pa could still identify his wife, it was not necessary to proceed with the other tests. You could see the many broken bones in her body from the accident. Her arms and legs had multiple fractures and were separated resulting from the movement of the casket. Her rib cage looked flat from the trauma of the accident. Her hair, for some reason, still looked good and she was wearing her favorite earrings that Pa gave her for an anniversary gift. As difficult as it was, this gave us another chance to say good-bye to Omz. We left Pa for some private moments and waited until we heard him weeping. It was time for a group hug, and that is what happened. There was nothing like family to help soothe the pain. Pa was there for us and we wanted to be there for him. When we left, I saw the workers and managers, as well as Barry, wiping their eyes. It was a huge moment for the family to go through. Mentally, we had to give her up all over again, as we hoped she would not be found in the casket.

Later on, Barry told Shawn that the temperature of the graveyard had to be optimum as with that type of trauma to a body, usually there would be no way to identify it after this length of time. Not even by skeletal remains. Pa would have seen the wedding band and the gold tooth no matter what the body looked like. Forensics was a powerful tool, but knowing someone personally and being intertwined with their lives often was a greater key. Barry told Dad and myself that the investigation would proceed full tilt, as now they knew who they were looking for. The story regarding Bella's phone call had a few discrepancies but they would get to the bottom of it. Andy still lived in the area and that would help the search.

Now we knew it was Omz in our graveyard. There was no denying it. She had really passed away in that horrible accident caused by Vinnie. Mark came over to the family and said he was so sorry that his uncle had caused this pain. Naturally, it was no fault of Mark's or Angela's. They were victims just like our family. Dad hugged Mark and said he did not want to hear him take ownership of that action or any other that Vinnie had made.

He was stern and said, "Did you hear me son? Did you hear me in your heart and head?"

Mark nodded, "Yes," and looked relieved.

I wondered if Dad realized, just how good he was for Mark? He sure knew how to encourage and set his mind on the right track.

Grammy and Grammpy prompted everyone to come into the house or sit on our porch and have some leftovers. She had fried chicken, potatoes, vegetables, preserves, homemade rolls, ribs and ham. She over did it by a long shot. The Amish Shoo Fly pie was good, although there wasn't enough for everyone so Grammy pulled out some pastries from her new freezer. We toasted to Grammy and Grammpy as a delightful addition. Every time we met as a family, it got better and better. There was more to talk about and more love to experience. Dad announced that we would have company from Germany very soon. His name was Dustin and he would be looking at the job situation in the area and a possibility of moving to Canada with his brother and mother. We would look forward to meeting the first of our ancestors from Europe.

Everyone helped with the cleanup and the day ended with some good vibes, even if it started with much apprehension.

CHAPTER 7

The Hunt is On!

It was time for another breakfast. The smell of bacon made its way up the stairs to my room. I noticed my foot was feeling much better this morning. I ran down the stairs supporting the ankle by holding onto the railing. Even Bee joined us this morning. We all sat around the table enjoying our bacon and eggs when Dad announced that tomorrow was a good time to try to find the hydro tunnels and hopefully the dynamite. We almost jumped off our chairs.

"Can I come this time, please?" pleaded Bee.

"Of course, you were always invited, only you were too busy," said Dad.

Bee agreed as she knew that was true, but delighted that she could go this time. Dad thought maybe Pa could stay here with Mom and the other grandparents and hold the fort while we were gone.

"Pa, we need someone here at home that knows all the information if we have problems of any kind. Is that alright with you?"

Pa replied that he didn't like it, but he would let them treat him like and old man, because he was the senior. He agreed that someone should stay behind, that had all the information and knew how to use it.

"I remember everything you have told me, Pa. I have copies of all the maps and so on. We have supplies in the tunnels below already. I think that was the toughest job of all. I think we will start out early tomorrow morning."

Just then the door opened after a quick knock.

"We smelled the bacon and wondered if you had extra?" Mac and Mark entered.

"Sure, sit down," said Mom.

Josh couldn't wait to tell his friends about tomorrow's excursion, not thinking that of course they would want to go too. They both looked at Josh's Dad, with pleading eyes.

"Now how do you think we are going to explain your absence to your parents? And will they let you go? Dad asked.

"We can go away and I can keep Bee occupied since she is so … lonely," said Mac.

"I can always go away with you guys. You know that!" said Mark.

Dad almost laughed, saying, "And where are we going to go?"

We all sat there and blurted out in unison, "Camping."

"We will pretend to go to Algonquin park where there is no phone service" Josh announced.

"Is this what you kids do all the time? Sit around and make up stories to cover yourselves? You seem to be very good at it," Dad chuckled.

Pa finally spoke up, "I think I remember a few times when you, Shawn–"

"This is not the time, Pa, please! I am trying to discourage them," Dad interrupted.

"Pa, tell us what Dad did?" Josh pleaded.

Pa replied, "Well now, I think I should respect your Dad's wishes as he is trying his best to raise you right."

"Thank you for the support." Dad added, "I will tell you what. We will have time to tell stories on the trip. You had better get permission from your parents and prepare your camping equipment. Only what you can carry on your backs. Okay girls?"

"We know, why are you talking to us?" Bee questioned.

"We will only take lip stick, Dad!" and she laughed.

"Bee hardly wears lip stick. She is what you call a natural beauty, like myself." Mac winked.

They jumped up to gather their equipment and got ready.

Mac and Mark hoped they would be able to go. They would text with their parents' answer. Pa asked where Grammy and Grammmpy were this morning. Nerissa said that they wanted to get into a routine and were having breakfast in their new place. Pa agreed that they should take advantage of their new surroundings and feel at home. She also reminded Pa that his schedule could be his own if he so desired. He agreed and already knew that, full well. He enjoyed the hustle and bustle of the family as long as he had his down time every day. He thought it was a good compromise, enjoying both.

Grammpy watched Mac and Mark walking up the laneway talking. Their hands were waving faster than the two were talking. He wondered what was going on this morning.

Mac's Dad, Barry, was going out of town to follow up on a lead regarding Bella. The police had posted a missing person report. After drawing a sketch according to Andy's direction, the police station received a lead. Barry would be away for at least four days. For this reason, he consented that Mac could take the opportunity to go camping. He thought that she would enjoy herself with the Wittfoot family.

Grammpy watched her run down the lane with a very full backpack. He wondered what the hurry was. Then he watched Mark come running out of his house with a whole load of stuff. He almost raced over to the mansion. Angela was delighted that he would get a chance to go camping. She couldn't provide that kind of entertainment for him, as she had to work and was continually short of money. She felt so blessed to have such good people around her.

Dad and the others would leave early in the morning. The car would be hidden in the garage and not moved.

CHAPTER 8

A Lost Soul

Barry was on his way to investigate his case. He was going to the town of Parry Sound to follow the lead. He was more than grateful that the black fly season was over. Or was it ever really over? Vanessa had packed him a great lunch and he would arrive at his hotel within three or four hours depending on the traffic. What would he find? He stopped for a coffee before he got to the Parry Sound Police station.

He received a report in response to the photo of Bella he posted and hoped that this trip would be somewhat successful. Hopefully she hadn't changed too much or was trying to hide and disguised herself. In any case, someone thought they had spotted her.

After doing business at the police station, Barry settled into his hotel room. He made his phone calls and was off again. He had a lead that the missing person was seen near the hardware store. There were many tourists that stopped in this area for groceries, and fast food and supplies. He would check the area out. He went into McDonald's and asked if anyone had seen this person, showing her picture to them.

"I have seen someone that resembled her," The manager contemplated, "She was going through the garbage outside. It looked like she was looking for food."

"Does she come by regularly?" Barry asked.

"I would say about twice a week," was the reply.

Barry continued, "When was the last time you noticed her?"

"Well, I have the same shifts every week, and it is mostly on

Wednesday and Friday that I see her. She comes in to use the bathroom, too. When I take the garbage out, she is sitting behind the garbage barrier and resting. She leaves when she sees me, but I never tell her to leave as she doesn't bother me! I am fortunate to be off on Saturday and Monday and wouldn't know if she comes by then."

"You have been very helpful, thank you."

"What has she done? Is she a murderer?

"I cannot discuss the case with you, but I can tell you that you and your establishment are in no danger. I will hang out here in order to speak with her if that is alright with you," Barry asked.

It was agreed that they would treat Barry like a customer so no attention was drawn to him. Since tomorrow was Wednesday he would return early in the morning. It was a successful day already, and Barry was making good use of his time. He would go to the shelter downtown and try to pick up some more leads.

The less fortunate were just checking in for their night's stay when he arrived. It was an appropriate time to be there. After speaking with the person in charge for the night, he discovered that yes, she had frequented this location but few and far between. She was not a regular. Barry waited until the cots were all taken. Sadness overtook him for all these people who did not have a home. Most of them had just hit on hard times and needed that little bit of extra help. They did not look like the type of people that made a life of depending on others to bail them out. They were probably too proud to ask for help and that is why they were here. They were going to make it on their own. Barry could appreciate that. He knew there were families and stories behind every face.

The next morning came early. Barry reread all his reports all the way back to the accident. He was missing something?

He made a call to the station back home. "I would like to know where Andy Shantz lived in the past and the dates. Call me as soon as you get that information, please."

He was on his way to have a coffee before waiting to see if Bella would show up at McDonalds. He spotted something unusual while driving. There was a woman, banging her head on a storefront, and she was bleeding. With blood running down her face, she was holding her head with both hands and looked like she was in terrible pain. Barry stopped the car and called for an ambulance. He grabbed the stranger and held her so she could not hurt herself anymore. Barry waited with her until the ambulance arrived. He tried to find out who she was, but she kept saying she didn't know and the pain in her head was tormenting her. He gave his information to the medics and left her in good hands.

Barry could see the way she was abusing her head. It was terrible and he wondered why. He would check in with her later but first he wanted to find Bella. He waited all day, had too many coffees, salads and burgers, not to mention all the newspapers he read. It was a long day. The walks to the dumpster area were refreshing but not productive.

"Well I guess you are out of luck today?" said the manger.

"Yes, I guess I am. Do you think she will still come by?" Barry wondered.

"No, she never comes this late," he suggested.

Barry thanked the manager for his support and gave him a business card. "Here is my cell number, please call me if you see her."

"Sure thing, will do," came back a positive reply.

Barry was wondering how the woman that he rescued this morning was feeling. She certainly wasn't coherent when he spoke to her earlier in the day.

He drove to the hospital and inquired, showing his badge. They directed him to her room as she had been admitted.

The nurse was standing between the patient and Barry. She asked her about the headaches and how long she had them.

She repeated herself over and over, "I don't know! I don't know! I don't know!"

Suddenly, Barry sensed someone standing behind him. He turned to see a slender well-dressed women waiting to enter the room. Barry especially noticed her big smile and white teeth as she said hello to him. He would walk out and give her time with the patient. Could she help this mysterious patient?

He stood outside the door and listened. The nurse left the room. The visitor spoke to the mystery patient as if she knew her.

"The hospital called me when they found my number on you. Did you have another bad episode?" She asked.

"I did and don't know what I was doing!" She cried, "What am I going to do, Jackie?"

Jackie reminded her friend of the things she had told her to help her in these kinds of situations. The woman in bed replied that she remembered, that the pain got so bad she blacked out. Jackie told her that it would be fine and they would figure it out.

Barry decided to join the two and see if he could help. He walked in and as the patient came into sight, he was shocked.

He recognized her immediately.

He addressed her, "Bella? Is that you Bella?"

Jackie, with a surprised look, questioned, "Is that your name? Bella? Bella, that is your name!"

Bella started to cry, "Yes, I think it is! My name is Bella!"

Barry was confused. Jackie filled him in on how she met Bella in need one day and took interest in her. She wanted to help her, but Bella was very elusive and kept disappearing. Bella did not know her name or who she was prior to coming to Parry Sound. Jackie wondered who Barry was, and was Bella in trouble. Barry informed her that we were looking for her in connection with a case but that she was not in trouble. We needed information.

"Bella, do you know an Andy?" Barry asked.

She couldn't place the name but somehow, thought she did. She was very confused.

Barry put her last name out there to see what the reaction would be. "Have you heard of the Shantz family?"

"That is my name!" She was ecstatic! Speaking with euphoric tones, "I know that is my name. I know who I am." She quickly added, "How will I find out about myself?"

Barry and Jackie both assured her that she would get the help she needed to recover her loss of memory.

"Can you remember anything at all?" Barry prodded.

"I have nightmares. They turn into terrible headaches. I see a boy. He is so small and always points at me. He always disappears in my nightmares. I cry during every one of these dreams as the horror of his loss overtakes me. I have nightmares where I am falling and think

I will die. The other dream that repeats itself is of a cruel man beating me until I think I will die."

Barry excused himself to make a call outside the room. He called Pa, as he knew Shawn was away.

"Can you pick up Andy and bring him to Parry Sound? I have found Bella, but don't tell Andy why he is coming. I think it will help her to recall her past. She has amnesia. "

Pa was shocked and replied, "Of course, if you think it will help get to the bottom of this mystery with Omz!"

Barry would send the address to have Andy picked up. Pa expected to arrive about ten in the morning at the hospital after their drive. He wouldn't be able to sleep all night thinking about it.

Barry returned, and Jackie was consoling Bella with the fact that she now knew who she was. The rest would reveal itself soon. Barry asked Jackie where she could be reached if the need arose. She was glad to give him her cell number. What are the chances that the woman he stopped to help was the one he was searching for? It felt like divine intervention.

It was too much to deny the miracle when Jackie asked Bella, "Do you know who has done this?"

Bella affirmed, "Yes I do. It was God, He heard my plea."

Barry felt like he was in the right place at the right time and with the right people. Everyone was in his or her special position, waiting for what God would reveal next! Barry wondered what Bella would remember when she saw her brother Andy.

Pa was anxious about the next day and thought how thankful he was that he was not in the tunnels with the others. Nerissa sensed how he was feeling and thought it would be a great idea if he asked Grammpy to accompany him. Grammpy had never been up that way and would enjoy the lovely scenery and conversation. Pa also enjoyed the companionship and did just that. Grammpy would be ready at five in the morning. This was not too early for the two seniors, as they grew up in the era where you took pride in how early you got up to start your day. As a matter of fact, they used to brag about it to their friends. When Pa called Andy, he was not so thrilled to leave shortly after five in the morning. Pa knew that he would be more than happy to go any time, if he was told the reason for the trip. Pa suggested he snooze in the car on the way up.

The plan was to leave early so a breakfast stop could be made. Pa loved going out for a good breakfast and Grammpy enjoyed it as much. They stopped along the highway at Angels before leaving the city. They served a great breakfast and it wouldn't be busy at that time of day.

Of course, the trip involved a coffee stop or two. Andy said he would just get to doze off when the elderly gentlemen would make a pit stop. He also insinuated that he was enjoying the trip very much. He let them know that he lived in Parry Sound as a little boy and had not been back since. This was such an unusual trip and he wondered why the police wanted him to go.

Pa just said," I guess we will find out soon enough."

After hearing Andy's story, Grammpy had compassion for him, too. He assured him that it was all meant to be and he should relax. He deserved a little trip and he should enjoy the ride. Nothing bad was going to happen. Andy was used to bad things happening to him. It was what happened over and over. Pa reminded him that he should expect good things to happen. He said it was a mind set. A way of life! Grammpy confirmed Pa's encouragement.

We were at the hospital and Pa texted Barry. Grammpy said he would have to get himself one of those phones, as they seemed so handy. Andy was very concerned as the first stop was the hospital.

Barry was at the elevator to meet them. Pa and Grammpy gave Andy and the officer time to connect. They waited down the hall as the two talked in the waiting room. Andy looked shaken as he neared the seniors after his conversation with Barry. Pa reminded him of how he should expect good things to happen to him. It brightened Andy's face. Barry took him into his sister's room. He asked Pa and Grammpy to give them a minute and then follow.

Andy slowly walked in. "Hello, Bella," he said.

She gasped and shouted, "Andy!"

He went over and threw his arms around her, hugging her tight. It looked like he would never let go of Bella. She did the same. It was amazing that the sight of her brother opened another door to the hidden memories in her mind.

They talked, yet not believing it was true.

Bella kept saying, "This is not happening, this is not real!"

Andy stopped her. "This is happening Bella, and we can expect good things to happen to us!"

Andy looked at the seniors, now in the room, for confirmation to his statement, and they nodded with approval. Barry was there to get information and wondered if now was the time, as Bella suddenly asked about her mother's health.

Barry began. "Bella, first of all, you are not in trouble. I need to ask you some questions. If you can answer them, it would be helpful."

Andy quickly added. "Don't be afraid Bella, they will not hurt you. They have helped me find you, didn't they?"

"I will try," she agreed.

CHAPTER 9

The Real Story

Barry asked if she remembered her childhood. She thought for a minute, as she was not used to knowing about herself. She remembered... when Andy was born... her mother... and how poor they were. She was hesitant recalling when she ran away from home and the man she met. Suddenly, she stopped. She did not want to go on.

"Bella, Mom got a call from you just before you disappeared." Andy coached, "Tell them what happened!"

She reluctantly started again. She had run away from home and had no, "Street smarts", as she called it. She found herself hungry and homeless. She had made her way hitchhiking to Niagara Falls. The plan was to cross the border illegally. Her idea was to get as far away as she could from home. Not from her loved mother and brother, but from poverty and misfortune. She met a man that bought her a meal and treated her like a queen. She moved in with Vinnie, as it gave her security. He had a water delivery business and was away much of the time. She was lonely and made friends. Vinnie did not want her to have any friends and he started to beat her and confined her to the house with no money, credit card or phone. He became angry and cruel. She didn't know how to become invisible enough, to stay out of the reach of his terror. She nursed her wounds at home and even wrapped her ribs after he broke them. After another beating, her arm was broken, and he took her to the hospital. Vinnie stayed with her the whole time so she could not expose what he had done to her.

When she first got to town, she met an elderly lady who gave her some money for food. She also gave her a small piece of paper with her phone number and address on it. This lady was kind and said it was up to Bella to call her.

Vinnie wanted Bella to help him kill someone. He did not say who it was. She refused and the beatings were intolerable. Bella decided to run away again and thought of the piece of paper she had carefully hidden. She took it and ran for her life. She knew if she were caught, it would mean death for her. She called the number and the lady answered. It was morning and the lady wanted to pick her up immediately. Bella refused, as she was so afraid of getting caught. She pleaded with the lady to meet her when it was dark. The kind woman was going to the Royal George Theater in down town Niagara –on-the- Lake that evening and she would meet her in the parking lot in the back. Vinnie would never suspect her to be there and it sounded safe. As they spoke in the parking lot, the lady who said she was known as Omz, reassured Bella that she had a place for her to stay and that she would be safe. As she clutched her stomach the elderly lady said she had a neighbor that was a police officer and that information should have helped Bella relax. Not being able to shake that sick feeling, the elderly woman started to vomit. She thought maybe it was food poisoning. Bella assisted the senior to pull herself together. She remembered the lady saying it was a good thing Bella had her wrap and purse, as they would have been a mess. Bella was asked to drive the lady's car for her, as she regained her composure. Bella activated the GPS to go home after the car started. Bella was told to take the ladies phone out of her purse and call whatever family she had and tell them all was well. The elderly woman said, if she was family, she would want to know that Bella was safe.

Bella recalled her phone conversation with her mother while driving. She had a difficult time as she sobbed and the tears blurred her eyes. She received a tap on the shoulder and Omz told her to stop the car. They changed positions while Bella was still on the phone. Bella did not fasten her seat belt, as she was too preoccupied. Omz told her to feel private in the back of the car, and she would try not to listen. The senior lady put the windows down to get fresh air. It helped her to feel better. Bella was telling her mother what a good life she expected to have and started to cry violently.

"Those words came from the depth of my soul," she remembered. "Suddenly we were hit with something and I felt wet. I don't know what happened but the car turned sharply towards the bank and started to go over the crest into a gorge."

Omz shouted, "Jump!" I must have? All I remember is that I hit my head on something. I felt stunned when I came to and didn't know what happened or who I was. I saw a culvert, just a few feet up the embankment. I heard noises and saw lights flashing. I crawled deep into the culvert and stayed there in the dark until the sirens left. It seemed to take forever. I did not know where to go, so I walked without purpose. First, a farmer going to the market picked me up. Then a trucker hauling cars took pity on me and gave me a ride. He was a nice man who shared the lunch his wife had made for him. I recall the fresh baked goodies and him telling me of how much she loved to cook and bake. I remember this because he said he wished I could meet her and she would teach me these things. I ended up in Parry Sound and somehow I could not leave here. I tried a couple of times.

"Does this mean I have to go back and face Vinnie?" she asked with a terrified look.

"No, you won't have to worry about that," Barry assured, "He is dead."

She looked so relieved. "How is Omz?"

Pa stepped up and introduced himself as the husband of Omz. He gently explained how she died and that there was a gnawing mystery to her death. Things did not add up.

She caught that Omz was dead, "Oh no... I killed her. She was taking me to a safe place. I killed her."

"No you did not!" Pa said. "She was going home; don't you remember the GPS was set on home? She would have taken that road no matter what. It was her favorite stretch of this area. "

"Vinnie would have been waiting for her, with or without you," assured Barry.

"Vinnie killed Omz? I didn't know who he wanted to kill, I swear! I would not have killed that nice lady. Please believe me!" she cried in anguish.

Andy held her as she cried, grieving the kind lady that gave her hope. She wondered why she had to die.

Pa added, "I am glad she had you in the car to worry about. I think it kept her mind focused on saving you, until her untimely end. We would never think less of you, but more, because my wife saw hope and change in you. She showed love and kindness to who you were right then and there."

It was rewarding for Pa, Grammpy and Barry to see the healing taking place. In just minutes, Bella's mind and spirit were healing.

Bella asked Andy, "Is Mom somewhere close by?"

"I'm sorry Bella, she passed away. Before she died I promised her that I would find you. She was so worried about you. It made her happy that you said your life was turning around and that is what she told everyone who would listen. Thank you for calling her," Andy sympathized.

Bella would be in the hospital for a while to make sure her recovery was completed. Andy wanted to stay with her but that would need to be figured out. He could stay with Barry for a night. Andy didn't leave much behind in Niagara. His life, as well as Bella's, was on the right track now and they were together again. Pa and Grammpy were going to make their way back home again. Andy and Bella gave them big hugs, as they were overwhelmed with gratefulness. Barry would pick up Andy later, with some dinner and then they would return to the hotel.

Barry called Jackie to give her a report on the days' activities. Bella had answered many haunting questions to what happened to Omz. She asked if there was anything that she could do, as she and her husband needed to come into town for supplies for the build of their new home. As they were stopping in to see Bella. Barry asked if she could supply Andy with one set of casual clothing as he was staying with Bella. She was glad to bring a complete set belonging to her husband. That would be easy.

The next day, Andy was dropped off at the hospital and Barry would stop in later. Barry made his reports and phone calls and the case of Omz's not so accidental death was over for good. It was too bad the lead did not surface before her body was exhumed.

When he arrived at the hospital, Jackie and her husband were already there and they were laughing. Bella had asked her brother why everything about him looked so pointed. Everything about him "was" pointed.

"Bella, you always called me, "Pointy!" He replied.

"Yes, but that was because you never stopped pointing at things and people. It became embarrassing."

"I thought I looked pointed to you and somehow was trying to keep my image up for your sake!"

"Come here, little brother, and give me a comb," she urged.

She made him look like a new man. His hair was combed to the side on top and back over his ears, falling just over the top of them. She commented how cute his nose looked. It was an attractive feature, separated from that bundled look he came in with. She also reminded him they would get rid of those shoes and buy some stylish ones, when she could afford it.

Barry commented on his new appearance and how fashionable he was looking. They decided that small changes can definitely enhance an image. Jackie and her husband were enjoying the whole bit of drama amongst the siblings. Barry asked if Jackie knew anywhere that Andy could stay in the area. He wanted to be close to his sister. He would also need a job if the siblings were staying in town. Jackie and her husband would let Barry know if they heard of something. After coming back from having a coffee, Jackie asked to speak to Barry privately, so they stepped outside the room to talk. They would hire Andy to help build their home, just out of town, and Bella could find a job when she was well. For now, if they wanted, they could stay in a trailer they have on their property. Barry was so thankful to them for putting his mind at ease before he left. Bella and Andy were good people and now would also be surrounded with good people to guide them along the way. Barry would stay in touch.

"Good–bye you two. Take care of each other. Jackie wants to talk to you about something after I leave and the decision is yours. I expect your lives will be different from here on in. If you ever get a chance to visit us, please do," Barry encouraged.

Jackie said to Bella," Well, do you know who planned this one?"

"Of course I do," Bella replied.

"It was God," Andy interjected.

"I guess we are all on the same page." Jackie announced.

Barry would be glad to get home and felt great satisfaction in finding the missing puzzle pieces. His friend and neighbor would sleep a lot better knowing what really happened. He knew he was just an instrument used to make this world a better place.

He couldn't imagine how Pa felt. He would have to have a coffee with him when he returned, to make sure he was dealing with the new revelations.

CHAPTER 10

Following the Old Map

Dad and the group started packing all our necessities in the underground living space. We recognized it might be a while to find the hydro plant tunnel. We had to get back within a five-day period or Mac and Mark's family would worry. We split up the necessary communal items and after that we could take whatever personal items we wanted to carry. We were excited and Dad wondered why he let himself be talked into this teen adventure. He felt like a Boy Scout leader. We all had high-powered but small size flashlights. Dad supplied us with a couple of cans of bear spray and some strong walking sticks as well. He had a taser gun for an emergency, just in case we ran into the wild cougar again. We went through the tunnels and down the stairs, to behind the bones of the ancestors. Bee had not been here before and was in awe of the place. We pointed out the hand of Friedrich, Pa's uncle, and Mark said he wished he knew which one was "his" relative. We reverently filed by like we were at a viewing in a funeral home. Quietly and somberly we strained to see if we could recognize someone. Not much of a chance of that, seeing we did not take much time.

The tunnel was large at this point and it made sense that it was so very deep. It extended beneath the ravine on the side of the house and probably connected the two sides of the gully. We were starting to talk again as we had entered well into the passage. Dad was in front and the girls between him and us boys, keeping them in the safe zone. What was it about the female species that made you want to protect them? Would we ever find out? Mark and I had a great time chatting about so many things: video games, Play Station, getting out of high school after this next year and weapons. The girls talked about hair products, makeup, the clothes they loved and that they would miss their friends. Dad, well he hummed himself a tune and just kept on walking. This was a long tunnel with no end in sight. Dad realized, after looking at the map, that it had crossed underneath the ravine, beneath the gazebo. There was no other way to get across and still be hidden.

We kept on following him. It was getting wet. We had all worn our rain gear, so a little water was just fine. Dad slowly felt the floor with his walking stick. He didn't want to end up falling into a hole filled with water. All quiet and paying attention, we were nervous about the water level rising. It was now up to our knees. We were almost going to turn back when we started to climb again. Now relieved to get out of the water, we smelled a horrid odor! What was that? We pulled our jackets up over our mouths and noses trying not to breath. Was it going to poison us? We were frightened at the unknown. Dad was moving quickly as he wanted to pass the smell too. It was getting unbearable. Finally, we saw the rotting carcass of an animal. How gross. All we could see was that it was large, like a cougar, as we hurried by to escape the stench.

We almost broke into a run, even though we were still climbing. The air was finally getting better the higher we went until we thought the smell was far enough behind us. You couldn't really tell, because it seemed to permeate our noses and linger there. It almost seemed like we could taste it. When we found a wide enough place to stop, we tried to take some good breaths of fresher air. Bee said she was going to be sick. Not so uncommon to feel that way, Dad acknowledged, saying that it was a terrible smell to endure. The animal must have gotten trapped with the water rising. But why didn't he or she leave to go the other way? We had nothing but questions with no answers.

"Let's see how far we can get today. I don't think anyone wants to eat anything quite yet, is that right? The lingering thought of that smell was still too fresh in our minds. I think we should have a drink to introduce a new flavor," Dad added.

"Copy that!" We all shouted.

Dad suggested we talk instead of shout, as we never knew if there were air tunnels, or what lay around the next corner.

"Good idea," agreed Mark.

"Are you trying to make points?" Mac added, knowing Mark was the loudest one in the group.

"No…" he replied.

Dad interrupted the deep conversation, (not) and told us to look around in case we came all this way and missed something. He told the girls to look on the right side and the guys the left. Dad would take the top and the bottom. It kept everyone busy for a while, until the girls decided they were thirsty again. We all stopped for a drink. The soda pop was so good and seemed to finally clean the smell out of our heads. Eating a few health bars when we were hungry, we chose not to stop for a meal. We kept on going, knowing the day was wearing on. Not that it mattered, as the light stayed the same; total darkness. Dad knew we were tired and wanted to stop relatively soon. After some time, we came to a small cavern. It looked hand dug or even blasted, as it contained many boulders. It had nothing else in it. They moved into it as the map directed. It certainly looked like they were on the right track, as the small cavern showed on their map. Soon they would get to a crossroads in the tunnels.

"Here we are. Look at your maps. You all have a copy. Do you see the split in the tunnel? Which way should we go?" Dad asked.

We all studied the map, not wanting to be wrong. We followed each tunnel. One led to what looked like a dead end. It was closer to the gorge edge and even looked like it had a line to the gorge.

The other kept on going to the far end. Dad suggested that we take the short one and get it looked after. It would be one less to investigate on the way back.

"It might be a good place to sleep for the night since there might be fresh air from outside of the tunnel. What do you think?" Dad asked.

Of course we agreed, as it had been a day of no events except for the putrid smell. We continued left, towards the gorge edge. The tunnel went down again and we hoped it was not full of water.

"So far, so good," uttered Bee.

"No… not again!" Mac sighed, being the first to reach the water covered floor of one section of tunnel ahead of them.

Dad poked his walking stick down into the water. There was no bottom to be felt. He tried further over and found no bottom.

"Be careful kids, please back up! I don't want anyone falling in here."

He tried to find ground in another area with no luck.

"Okay, one more and we are done."

He started on the other side and poked into the water. He was almost shocked when the stick clunked and was stopped by the bottom. It sounded like wood only six inches down in the water. He tried another six dips in different areas and they were solid. One side seemed good with a wood bottom and the other treacherous.

"It is either trying to cross over the water or walk another couple of hours. What do you say?" He couldn't believe he had just said that.

"Let's go." Said Mac.

"Which way, Mac?" Josh asked.

"Forward, don't you think?" She replied.

We all agreed. Dad would have to work on the plan first. The boards that were covered with water extended only two feet from the wall. The height was only five feet high above the walkway. They would have to be careful not to hit their heads and lose their balance, which could cause them to fall into the deep cold side of the bottomless water section. Dad took out his rope and would be the first to cross. He would fasten it somewhere if he could and if not, hold it himself. Someone would take the rope and hold it on both sides. They would let the person crossing hold onto it in case they fell or the floor gave way.

"You can slide our back- packs across with that handy loop you brought, Josh," he said as he tied the rope to himself.

"Now Josh, you and Mark hang on to this tightly as I make my way over. This is just in case the floor caves in."

"We are ready," they agreed.

"Here we go!" he said as he stepped forward.

The girls almost held their breath. Dad took one step at a time, checking if there was solid floor ahead before he put his weight on it. He took small steps and kept close to the edge, ducking his head when necessary.

Everyone breathed a sigh of relief when he reached the other side. "Okay, send the back packs over one at a time."

He crouched so they could zip line the packs across the gap. It worked very well and they had them across in no time.

"Okay girls, you are next. It is your job to come over slowly while hanging onto the rope tightly. You must never let go. Always have a firm grip on the rope."

"Okay Dad, are you trying to scare us on purpose?" Bee asked.

Bee went first and had a very firm grip on the rope. She also took her time and slowly shuffled across. It seemed like she made it to the other side in no time. Bee seemed relieved and looked at her hands. She was definitely hanging on tight, too tight, as they were sore and red.

It was Mac's turn and she knew what to do. She moved forward and methodically worked her way across. She was almost there and looked confident when she bumped her head. It startled her and she panicked and almost jumped. We heard a board crack.

Dad told her to be calm and keep on coming as she was almost there.

She was so exasperated by the time she had crossed, that she stamped her feet.

She said, "No... I hope I didn't crack the board?"

"Mac, settle down, listen to me! It will be all right. Do you hear me?" Dad asked.

"Yes..." she answered hesitantly.

"Who's going next, boys?" Dad needed to know.

Josh gave the rope to Mark to hold and took a few steps and came back.

"See, it is okay to cross, Mark." Josh urged, "You go first."

"Do you have one of those clips to put onto the rope and onto Mark's belt?" Dad questioned Josh.

"Sure I have one, Dad," searching his pocket.

It was safely attached to Mark's belt.

Mark reported he was ready and stepped out into the water. He made his way slowly and steadily and made the crossing with no problem. It was Josh's turn next. He tied the rope to his waist and then started across. Everyone was nervous. One step at a time, he maneuvered his way across until almost to the other side. The board cracked and gave way as he threw himself in a diving position to the other side, sliding into Mark's feet. They had made it. Now how were we going to get back? We would deal with that later. For now, we had experienced enough excitement and wanted some food and rest. We picked up our gear and proceeded. Dad was leading again and we were close behind. It seemed to take much longer than we had expected. It always did for some reason or other. We felt a draft again and knew we were getting closer to the edge. We breathed deeply and it felt so good.

Dad shouted, "Here we are! It's beautiful!"

We hurried to see what he saw. Bee took ownership and declared this as her own place. It was so quiet with the moon shining high overhead. An open roof over thirty feet high gave way to a blanket of twinkling stars far above. It looked like a very deep crater with a diameter of approximately fifteen feet.

"Look over here!" Mac almost whispered.

"Why are you whispering?" we asked.

"Come and look," she waved.

It was an awesome sight. There was Girl with Sweetheart, lying in the moonlight. Girl knew we were there but looked at us with a… "Don't wake the baby," look.

We just marveled at how beautiful this place was. You could build a fire and no one would see it. The grassy ledge was a good size, filled with trees and wild shrubs. It almost made us jealous of Girl and Sweetheart, being able to wander these tunnels and find these small sanctuaries for themselves.

We had a bite to eat and then got our spots ready for night. We couldn't help but go outside and enjoy that beautiful view. Bee took pictures of the cougars to show Pa. She was reminded to be careful so no one else except Mom would see them. She promised. Down below in the distance, they viewed a boat docked for the night. The waves danced like a "Mosh" party moving every which way, crashing into each other violently. Josh and Mac couldn't help themselves from sitting a moment and reminiscing of the first time they saw such a magnificent view, under the same bright huge moon. This time, it was even quainter. It was a larger ledge and more treed. The vegetation caused shadows that swayed on the rock wall of the gorge, causing a stunning backdrop. They were reminded of how Girl could have killed them and she was now like family. Of course the cougar and her cub completed the piece of paradise they were fortunate to be in.

CHAPTER 11

The Goodnight Kiss

Dad made sure we were all in our sleeping bags before he put the lights out. Girl came in to check on us. We were all in our sleeping bags, quiet and eyes closed. Girl came to each of us as if she was tucking us in. She sniffed at our hair a couple of times and went to the next person. Bee was last and held her breath at this unusual moment. Bee loved the little sniff and lick on the cheek. After that, Girl went outside where Sweetheart was sleeping. We talked about Girl's actions awhile and just couldn't get to sleep right away. Bee felt very honored, as she got a goodnight kiss as well as a tuck in sniff. Who else in the world experienced a tuck in and kiss from a cougar?

The next morning, we found our bodies stiff from the hard ground and stretched to get going. The cougars weren't there anymore and we looked around not knowing how they got off the grassy ridge. It certainly wasn't visible to us. After a little breakfast and packing up, we were off.

Of course, much consideration had been given to the water that we would have to cross again. That would be figured out later. Dad was in charge and would get us across. He was quiet and seemed nervous, and we wondered if he was concerned. After arriving, we saw a light in the pool. There was daylight coming into the water from below somewhere. We could not figure it out, but then noticed a hole in the cave ceiling where the light shone in. This was odd. The shape was exactly the same as the light shape in the pool.

"Dad, could it be a mirror?" Josh asked.

"I don't know yet!" he replied.

Mark and Mac got on their knees and looked closely at the water with their flashlights. "Yes, it is a mirror," they both shouted! It is reflecting the light from above." Josh and Bee were also on their knees by now and Josh took the walking stick to see if he could feel the mirror. Yes, he was able to touch it. It sat on the bottom of the rock floor of the pool and was tilted just right, to reflect the light. But why, was the question.

"It sure helps us to see this is not an endless pit of water!" Bee said.

"Even if we fell in, we would not drown." Mac got off her knees, "I wonder what is under the board side?"

"Good question, let's find out," commanded Mark.

Bee and Dad moved to the opposite side of the boards and tried to look under the water and boards, with no luck.

"I have a mirror if you want it?" Bee asked, holding it out.

Dad looked at her and said, "You were supposed to pack light! In any case, it was good of you to bring it."

"You're welcome!"

Dad held the mirror at an angle under the water and shone the light under the boards. It looked like the boards were only a couple of inches above a rock ledge. Dad thought we would have to come back when the rainwater had drained away and check out if we could see more. The rest of us protested.

"Look Dad, it is only about oh…less than ten inches deep. We can see what is under that."

Dad agreed, and we slowly walked over the boards to the other side. The water had already receded and now was only a couple of inches above the boards. We could see the one that was cracked and could avoid it. Our backpacks were on the rock floor and Dad started to take the boards off. They were just laid there and slightly tacked down to keep them from floating. Easily removed, we carefully put them aside to put back later. There was a cutout in the rock shelf that held a small rusty metal box. After retrieving it, we were curious as to its contents. We gave Dad some room and he worked at the rusty latch. I took out my pouch and dug through it for something to pry it open. It had no lock, just a rusty latch. The small screwdriver I found worked to loosen and lift the latch up. Dad maneuvered the screwdriver all the way around and finally loosened the rusty top enough to open it. We huddled close to get a look. It was old paper. We took out the wrinkled damp pieces of paper very carefully. There in the bottom, in a small block of wax, was a key.

"What an ingenious idea!" exclaimed Dad. "The wax sealed the key from moisture so it couldn't rust. I see the wax was also around the edge of the tin box. That is why the paper wasn't soaked."

Mac and Bee were examining the papers. There was a faint picture of a huge door. We all examined the paper. Other than the drawing, we saw nothing. Dad told us to take it and keep it somewhere safe. Bee thought her wallet would work well.

Dad, seeing her wallet, inquired "For what and where were you going to shop?"

"You never know when you need your identification, Dad!" she sneered in jest.

"I guess you're right."

She took the paper and carefully put it in her wallet for safekeeping. They moved on happily after Josh reminded his Dad how important it was to check everything out before moving on. Josh was sure this would be an important find for some time in the future. It was one of those very old keys and larger than the ones we have for our homes, and it was heavy.

We made good time and walked for a couple of hours. After our break, Dad looked at the map again. It looked like we would have to walk another couple of hours if the proportions were correct, but one never knew how accurate the maps were. We moved ahead with nothing exciting to stop us.

"Are you remembering to check out your designated sides?" Dad asked.

"The girls are," Bee boasted.

"The boys are now," Mark confessed.

They got to the larger part of the tunnel. This was getting close to the power plant. They should soon be near it. There was no sign of dynamite. They looked around the perimeter of the small cavern-like area, setting it apart from the tunnel. Their flashlights scanned and scanned but there was nothing new to discover. Dad thought they should have a bite to eat, so they sat on the cold floor. Bee noticed the floor had straight ridges. We all jumped up and shone the lights on the floor.

"Look," Mac said standing beside Bee.

"It starts here and goes over there," she said, pointing.

"Well, will you look at that," came out of Dad's mouth.

I looked at him and he knew just what I was thinking. He was becoming Pa. Not that I minded, as Pa was one of my most favorite people.

He took his light and followed the line from start to finish, ending at the wall. He knew nothing was by chance so far and this would not be either. They had checked the wall already and found nothing. Bee was still looking at the floor and noticed something strange.

"Dad, check this out."

He hated to be interrupted, but went over to have a look. They were on their knees feeling and examining one small area.

CHAPTER 12

The Key and Dynamite

Dad announced, "I think we are going to try our key."

Everyone looked shocked and came over to have a look at the floor. He pointed out the keyhole and asked everyone to get their stuff together and get their backpacks on.

"You never know how these doors open, so you will have to stay close together," he warned.

They were antsy and nervous, not knowing what was going to happen. He turned the key and they all stood holding their breath. The floor started to lower. He turned the key the other way and it came up again.

"Okay, now we know we all have to stand on this section of the floor."

"Hang onto your flashlights very tightly," warned Josh.

Dad turned the key again and they were lowered down into who knew where? We made a circle of flashlights, not even realizing it. It was a protective mode to immediately see our surroundings. Mark reported that there was a tunnel right in front of him. Dad asked if anyone else had something to report. No one did, so they all stepped off at the same time. "We have to see if it will get us back up, before I pull the key out," warned Dad.

"Dad, stay on it and after going up and then down again, take the key out to see what it does. If it goes up, you can use the key to get back to us."

"Good idea, Josh!" Dad agreed.

That is what he did. Nothing happened. The elevator floor stayed down. They decided to sit there awhile to make sure it stayed down, just in case.

The next step was to check out the only exit down there. The tunnel was roomy enough and just high enough to walk and not hit your head. Much lower than the room we had just been in with the elevator. You would not want a basketball player to spend much time down here, it would be too hard on his back to hunch over continually. We only walked a few minutes and around a couple of corners when we came upon a room. It was large and filled with boxes.

Dad said, "This is it gang."

"What now, Dad?" wondered Josh.

"No one has anything that will start a fire, right? We will put our backpacks out of the way." Dad asked seeing the contents of the room.

"This one says, '*Dynamit!*'"(German for dynamite). Dad suggested it was very dangerous and even the old damp dynamite could explode.

What would we do? Dad ordered us to leave and get out of there. It was way too dangerous. He could not have us there any longer. The feeling of urgency took over the group and we were so focused on the dynamite that we didn't even look around. Mac was the one who noticed the tunnel. I said to head for it and we would get out of there. It was quite long and we hurried as if our lives depended on it. We could go no further. There was a huge steel door.

"Now this looks like the door that was on the sketch," announced Mac.

"You're right," Mark said.

Dad's hands went for the key and placed it into the obvious keyhole. The door opened! We almost cheered! It was a flat heavy door with huge bolts. The heavy looking structure had a very large steel ring to grasp while opening it. Dad used every bit of energy he had to pull the massive door open. Walking into the doorway, we realized it was part of the power plant. I don't know how many stories down, but it was definitely further than we had imagined. This was the generating plant.

"Stand behind me, away from the wall and door," Dad ordered.

He took a photo of the door from the plant side and more of what he could see in the plant.

There were numbers above the door so he took a close-up of that. "Let's go, kids."

Dad closed the door and we left. He hurried us through the dynamite cavern to the elevator. He stayed to take pictures of the contents. When he met us at the elevator, he inserted the key and turned it. We rose up to the floor above and got off. I could tell Dad had a plan. He said he was going to send pictures to the electric company and hopefully they would secretly take care of the dynamite. Once the elevator was up it looked like the rest of the rock surface and no exit would be visible from the bottom. It would look like the tunnels stopped.

Dad filled us in on his thoughts. The professionals would have no problem dealing with this much dynamite, although they might wonder why it was old German dynamite, until they researched their old documents. They might see my Grandfather, Herbert Wittfoot's name. He was investigating the plot and had discovered it. Afterwards he was accused of being a spy and taken off of the case because he was a suspect.

Josh said with pride, "Well we finally proved the Germans had a plan, didn't we?"

"We sure did, son," Dad said with an arm around Josh's shoulder. The only problem is how to clear Herbert's name without releasing all the facts.

Everyone was elated that we had found the dynamite. We would be out of danger in a short while. On our way back towards home, we arrived at the crossroads tunnels, where the one passageway led to the water pool.

Bee reminded Dad of the fact that they did not put the boards back and they should do that. He knew why she wanted to go back and decided one night was too short a camping trip and they would spend another night in the tunnels. Excited, we hurried to get back to one of our favorite destinations in the tunnels. We were not afraid of the water anymore, as the discovery of its depth was made earlier. It took no time and we arrived in the magical open topped rock formation. Of course, our first move was to see if Girl was there with her young. She wasn't there, and everyone was disappointed. It would not be quite the same but we would enjoy this one of a kind place for one more night. Bee wished Kelly could see it, too. What would he say to all their secrets?

Dad made camp and opened some pork and beans for the kids. They were not going to make a fire as it was the nicest night and they didn't even need their jackets. The breeze made perfect conditions to keep the bugs away. The moon was one night short of being full. It was a beautiful night. The group took their food outside and sat talking and eating. Dad enjoyed listening to our chatter. He would try to bring Mom here some time. She would enjoy this place of solitude. Too bad it was not closer to home. It would make a great reading place or meditation area.

CHAPTER 13

Unexpected

Dad was inside the rock structure when company arrived. It was Girl carrying a very young kitten by the neck. She walked right by him and went straight outside with Sweetheart following her. She proceeded to where Bee sat. Everyone was startled. She carefully placed the malnourished kitten in Bee's lap.

"Oh, Girl, what do you have here?" She asked as if Girl would answer.

Dad followed Girl out with a first aid kit but the little body didn't seem hurt.

'Look what she gave me, Dad," Bee said.

Josh said he would get his canteen with milk. Mac had a small plastic bag with snacks. The bag might make a funnel. Mark had a heavy elastic band to put around the bag and plastic water bottle. Bee just held the kitten as Girl and her cub watched. Girl would lick the little fragile kitten, as if to say, "Come on keep on trying. "

The cougar was starved. Bee started to pour some milk into its mouth from the makeshift funnel. Of course she got it all over its face, but that didn't matter.

Dad said, "Take it easy Bee. Just give her a little at a time."

The cub didn't seem to have the energy to care about what was happening to her. Bee stopped for a while and wrapped her up in her jacket. She seemed to be lifeless.

"Dad, can we keep her?" she pleaded.

"Bee, you know she belongs in the wild, unless she chooses to let us into her life, like Girl."

Mac was beside Bee, petting the newly arrived patient. Mark wondered from where Girl got the cub. Dad figured it had been born on the other side of the tunnel, where we walked through the water on the way here.

Maybe with the rain, the parent left her cub behind to hunt. The rain must have filled the tunnel and she couldn't get back to its kitten. I knew a strong instinct would keep the parent there, until it could retrieve its cub. Where was the parent now?

"I will stay up and try to feed her every two hours or so," Bee said.

"Can I help you?" Mac asked.

"Sure, I will need all the help I can get."

Mark quickly remarked. "Well in that case, I guess we will all stay up."

Dad came back with, "speak for yourself, I am going to sleep."

Bee motioned and told Girl that she would take the kitten into their sleeping quarters. As she got up with the almost lifeless bundle, she carried it to her sleeping bag and snuggled up with the kitten, to keep it warm. Girl followed and licked the kitten before returning outside to lay down with Sweetheart. The kids put the sleeping bags close together so they could share the feeding. Dad was amazed that Girl would entrust this little stranger with the family. Dad told his group that Girl was still nursing Sweetheart and if they could revive the new arrival, Girl might also let her nurse at the same time. They usually nursed from 3 to 4 months, although the cougar would be taking Sweetheart and teaching her skills she needed for hunting. Young cougars usually stayed with their parents for approximately two years. Most adults lead solitary lives until mating season.

The kids were so interested in learning about the starved cub.

Bee decided after an hour to try some more milk. She could hear it go down into the cub's stomach with gurgles.

"At least it is going down," she whispered.

Afterwards she snuggled up with the kitten and dozed off. In an hour, Mac snuck the cub out of the sleeping bag and fed her some more milk. She quietly put it back. Bee ad Mac had discussed a name.

They figured they might as well give the cub a name, and it was going to be Halfpint. Josh and Mark took a turn the next hour to feed Halfpint. Dad suggested they let the cub rest and that it should have had enough for a few hours. They all fell asleep. Bee was startled, as some movement aroused her! It was Halfpint searching for food. She was regaining her strength and was hungry. Bee took the bottle to give her a little more milk. The cub would not stop drinking and finished it all. Bee asked if anyone had any more milk. No one had any left. They wished they would have saved some. Dad suggested that cub was on its way to recovery and the next step would be to see if Girl would accept her as her own.

"We will wait until she is hungry again," he suggested.

It laid stretched out against Bee for warmth and went to sleep. Bee took advantage and closed her eyes too. Everyone got a few good hours of sleep until Halfpint wanted some more food. They all got up to see what would happen. Girl was lying with Sweetheart near the rock ridge just outside the sleeping area. Bee took the cub over and put her with Girl. It wanted to follow Bee as she stepped back. Bee put her back beside Girl and Girl started to groom her. She seemed to clean every inch of the cub until she was satisfied that the kitten was clean, or was it to transfer her scent? We did not know. Halfpint found her food source and started to indulge. We were so proud of this wild cougar, our family friend, Girl. She truly had the instinct of a great parent. She not only cared for her own young but was willing to adopt one that was abandoned or lost.

Dad informed us, "This is a big step, as many adult cougars, male or female, kill their young and eat them. It was not so uncommon!"

We were startled with that and even more impressed with Girl. Sweetheart and Halfpint lay down beside Girl after feeding and looked like one big happy family. We were standing, just staring when Dad announced for us to get our stuff together and that we were moving on. With great reluctance, we did as we were told.

"Can I take some more pictures of the cougars?" Asked Bee.

She couldn't help herself and as she took a couple of photos of the three snoozing the morning away. She went to pet them all and could hardly tear herself away. Mac took a shot of Bee without her knowing.

We all called her, as Girl opened her eyes and looked to see what was going on.

"Okay. Okay. I hear you," Bee spoke annoyed.

She took one more look around at this piece of heaven. Nature and man in communion, interacting as if this was natural. Dad figured we could make it back to our underground living room by tonight and get back up to daylight in the morning. That, of course, was if there were no more surprises. They were happy at all they had experienced that weekend. If only they could talk about it with others. What great stories they would have to tell.

"Dad, what are you going to do about the dynamite? I mean, about figuring out how to get rid of it?" Josh asked.

"That question is still a mystery. I don't think they will send us a notice saying the job is done, or on hold, do you?"

Josh and the others chuckled at the thought, knowing that would not happen. Their mood was light and they made good time. They were nearing the decaying corpse and were ready. They left some t-shirts out to tie around their heads, covering the nose and mouth. It would be more comfortable, that was for sure.

They got to the corpse and were amazed that it was a little more than a skeleton.

"How could this be?" sighed Mark.

"Some kind of animals must have cleaned it up!" replied Josh. "Or maybe it was more than one."

"How do they stand the smell?" Asked Bee with a confirmation from Mac.

Dad looked at the remains with his flashlight, as we stood back. There were two bullets inside the rib cage and one in the head. He announced that this animal had been shot and that it must have been Half-pint's mother. The remains of the tail made it clear that it was a cougar.

The girls expressed their fear for the family friends.

Bee almost got tears in her eyes as she said, "Do you think Girl and her young are in danger?"

Dad didn't think so as she traveled deep within the tunnels and seemed to know where to hunt on the sides of the gorge. We hoped they would be safe.

We moved on and found that we did not have to travel through any water, as it had totally disappeared. It was frightening to think that when it rained, some of the tunnels filled with water. Instead of stopping, we kept on going until we were back at the shrine of skeletons. Walking past Friedrich's hand, Mark again asked if we knew which one was his relative?

Dad replied, "No, I am so sorry Mark, I don't know. Let's look at those photos when we get back and examine them very closely. Maybe there will be something that distinguishes him from the others?"

Mark felt a little better. It seemed to mean a lot to him to find his ancestor.

"Do you know, that I am the only one, that does not have a relative down here?" Mac spoke.

"Would you rather know that a relative of yours had to die here, in such a horrible way?" Josh asked with unusual insight.

"Of course not! I just mentioned it because you are all connected, having history in common," she said sadly.

Josh answered her with compassion in his voice. "I know it sounds odd, but the fact that you are a part of this discovery from the beginning is huge. You are a part of bringing justice to these descendants and giving meaning and value to their death! You are righting a terrible wrong that was dealt to them and their families. You are just as important as the rest of us."

Dad affirmed. "You will understand and be appreciated so much, when you meet the ancestors and see what this means to them."

"Well for sure, it has been an awesome experience," she returned a smile.

"Dad you said we would meet the ancestors?" asked Bee. "When and where?"

"It is not time yet as we have not found everyone." Dad replied. "I will let you know as soon as I do."

It sounded exciting and we wondered how we could do that without giving our secret tunnels away. We marched up the stairs in single file, tired from the hike. Our adrenaline was crashing as the trip was over. The underground living area looked so inviting. There were only three cots, so of course, the girls and Dad each got one. The boys stretched out on two furs from the wall as cushions and used their sleeping bags. We decided to eat later and just take a rest. Unknowingly, we slept all evening and all night until five in the morning. We decided to go upstairs soon afterwards and secretly arrive home before the world awoke. That way no one would see that the car did not come down the driveway, but was just backed out of the garage. Mac wondered how her Dad's business trip went. She would find out soon enough. Josh wondered if the grandparents had a relaxed time and if the moms spent all day getting their hair or nails done. Bee was anxious to connect with Kelly and wanted to make sure he got home safely. She was anxious as she wanted to tell him about Halfpint, but of course couldn't. Life was getting unbearable not being able to confide in her best friend. He knew she loved him and he loved her. She had never wanted to start a relationship with secrets. She made up her mind to speak to her mother about this. She was understanding and knew how to handle every situation.

They quietly went up the den entrance through Pa's office, then made their way to the kitchen.

There were homemade cookies on the table with a note, "In case you come home, have a snack." They sat down and devoured them.

"Do you know we forgot to have supper last night?" whispered Mac.

"No, we slept through supper last night," retorted Mark.

Dad interjected, "Okay guys, not to worry, we will make up for it at breakfast. Go and quietly wash up and I will start breakfast for you."

They left with their mouths full of cookies. Dad washed up at the kitchen sink. He started to mix the pancake batter and got out the eggs and sausages. He hoped his help was coming back soon.

"Well what can I do for you?" Asked Mac, being the first one back.

"First, you set the table and then fry the sausages."

"Great," she replied.

Bee came in before Mac was done setting the table and started to fry the sausages. The boys pushed through the door forgetting that everyone else was sleeping.

"Sh...Sh," said Dad.

Josh figured that everyone would be up as soon as they smelled the breakfast. Dad agreed but he wanted it to be their choice, not that they were rudely woken.

"The pancakes are almost done and so are the sausages. Someone start the eggs, please." he directed.

Josh fried the eggs and was getting so good at making perfectly fried sunny basted eggs. Mark took charge of the toast. Dad looked with pride at the kids, who were quickly turning into responsible adults. He sipped and enjoyed his pre- breakfast coffee but enjoyed his company even more. They sat down to enjoy the food they had prepared. Everyone was starved. Thinking about how hungry she was, Bee thought of Halfpint and how she must have felt. She smiled and everyone noticed.

Mac asked, "What is that smile about?"

"I was just thinking about Halfpint."

"What is half pint?" said Mom, as she entered the kitchen with Pa close behind.

"Oh boy, just what we have been waiting for, someone to tell our story to," Dad proclaimed.

As everyone started talking all at once, Dad asked, "Who wants to start?"

Everyone was quiet and laughed. Mom asked if we could take turns and tell them one at a time. The adults had to remind the teens a couple of times in order to understand what they were saying. Mom and Pa were so surprised about Girl bringing the small starving cub to Bee.

"Don't be so surprised," blurted Bee.

Pa was curios about how the cougars were doing and of course about the explosives.

Dad relayed his idea of notifying the authorities anonymously and let them take care of it.

Bee remembered her pictures and showed them. Everyone was in awe of how beautiful the ridge was and how healthy the cougars looked. Of course, the new addition was cooed over, and the photo was examined closely. Mac took out her phone and said she had a special shot. It was of Bee and cougars before she had to leave them. It was an awesome shot of Bee doing her thing with cougars. Bee was sitting with the trio and petting the youngest with Girl looking right up into her face, showing Girl's beautiful eyes. Mom said it was nice enough to enter into a contest, but we could never do that.

"Can you send it to me, Mac?" Bee pleaded.

"Sure I will do it right now," Mac replied her fingers in action.

"You will have to delete all of those photos. That goes for every-one." Pa demanded.

"Pa, I want to put them on my computer, on a disc and then de-lete, okay?" Bee pleaded emphatically.

The adults agreed and gave the okay. Mac knew she would have to delete hers as her Dad was suspicious enough already and a shot like that would put him over the top.

It was an interactive time sitting at the table having breakfast.

"Well, what is our next move?" Josh asked.

As Dad was reading his text he relayed, "I am afraid we will not have much time before we get company. Dustin has texted me saying he will arrive tomorrow as they have had a slowdown in their work schedule and he would like to visit now. Well, that was quick wasn't it? He is such a nice young man and you kids will enjoy hanging out with him."

"Does he speak English?" Mac asked

"Oh yes, he is very fluent in English. He took it in school," Mom replied and added, "I will get the guest room ready today."

Someone will pick Dustin up from the Toronto Pearson Airport tomorrow morning. Dad had to take care of some finances as he was being paid for some gold they had sold. It was going into an account in Europe. It was easier to make the change once to another country, in-stead of into Canadian currency first. The gold was almost all sold. All we knew was that it took a lot of work and we knew no other details. Some day they would have to tell us how all of this was done.

CHAPTER 14

A New Romance

The rest of the day was relaxed except for Mom, who was running around cleaning, making beds and so on. That is what moms are supposed to do, isn't it? I figured that this was why I and the others had such a relaxed life. Mom did all the prep work that no one else thought of doing. I also noticed that she always seemed to give the impression that it was no work at all, when the guests arrived or the party was ready to start. Moms were kind of like super women.

Dad had given us a picture of Dustin and he wasn't mistaken. His auburn hair and clear complexion together with his height made him a striking young man. He looked a little tired but was enthusiastic and excited to be in Canada. He only had his carry-on.

"A man after my own heart," Pa said looking at Dustin's one and only bag.

We embraced to welcome him as it just seemed right. After all, Mom and Dad had told us about their visit with Dustin's family. He texted his family that he had arrived safely as he imagined how relieved his mother, Mary, would be. It was easy communicating with him and we felt like friends in no time.

He filled us in on their business and home life. To hear his perspective on the discoveries in the home's basement was even better than Dad and Mom's version. We reminded him not to speak of it to anyone except our immediate family, excluding Grammy and Grammpy. We did not want people asking about the connection between those tunnels, Dad and Mr. Schwartz, Dustin's ancestor.

"I vill be varry careful," he said, rolling his "r".

When we arrived home, we wanted to give him a snack, but he wanted to get some sleep. He was shown to his room and we did not see him until after three. Carly was visiting Bee and staying for supper. They were going over some of their classes for this fall that they would be sharing. When Dustin came into the room he and Carly seemed to have chemistry. They couldn't seem to stop looking at each other. Bee introduced her friend and he shook her hand. It was the European way. As Dustin left to go to the kitchen after excusing himself, Carly expressed how her heart was fluttering!

"That guy is so cute!" she announced.

"I think he thought you were too!"

"Do you think so?" Carly prodded.

Dustin came back with a drink in his hand and they enjoyed the conversation, getting to know who he was. He told them of the family's plan to move to Canada if all went well and he could see his way clear.

"What will you do with the family home?" Bee wanted to know.

"I think we will keep it in the family," adding that they had many memories connected with that home. They would not have the finances to buy another one and that is why they had to secure work before they moved to Canada.

"How long are you staying?" asked Carly.

"I am not so sure," he answered. "It will depend on what I find here."

Mom was making dinner and Bee went to help her. Of course Carly wanted to help too, but Bee asked if she would entertain Dustin. She did not mind at all.

Dustin had told Dad that the museum wanted to set up tours in their home. It could be kept by them and the museum would pay rent for the use of the it. It sounded good to them. It meant that others would be able to see the dedication and sacrifice that was made, to experience what people now take for granted. The visitors to the home would be fascinated with the tunnels and artifacts that were saved, as well as the many books. Their tour would end with the dramatic visual of the small family hiding and sacrificing their lives instead of giving up the precious artifacts. Mitchell, Dustin and Mary were very excited about this happening. It could not be done while they were living in the house, so the sooner they moved, the better. They were so pleased that they could keep their home, just as it was, and it would be part of the museum. They would keep two bedrooms locked as part of their private area when they visited.

Carly asked if he had plans and if he would like to look around Niagara Falls or Niagara on the Lake the next day.

He thought about it and said he would enjoy that, if he had no leads on jobs to check out.

Pa and Dad walked in.

"*Guten Tag*," (Good Day) said Pa, practicing his German.

"Hello," said the guest in perfect English.

They got acquainted, and Bee called them in to eat. Grammy and Grammpy were coaxed to join them, as they should meet the guest.

The meal was delicious with lots of small talk. Mark burst in at the same time as knocking. He was anxious to meet this new guy from Germany. Their ancestors were friends and maybe they would have that same opportunity.

"Sit down Mark, and have some dinner," Mom invited.

He was already getting a plate and cutlery to join the them. Carly looked at him in surprise and thought he had some nerve. Pa noticed and casually mentioned that Mark was a member of the family and only slept elsewhere. They all laughed, and Carly understood. It was easy to fit into this accepting family. Everyone felt at home here.

"I have some leads for you to follow up on, if you want to start tomorrow?" asked Dad.

"Of course I would like to," Dustin said, looking at Carly.

"We can hang out after you are done," she said giving him her text number. "Just text me."

"Yes, thank you, I will do that," he responded.

Grammy and Grammpy were enjoying their new space with their family. Grammpy was wondering how Andy and Bella were doing and had anyone heard from them?

"I got a text from Andy this morning. He said Bella was going to be released tomorrow and he and Bella had a nice place to stay, right on the property where he was working. He thanked you Pa and Grammpy, for taking him up to see his sister. He was still overwhelmed at the fact that Barry found her. He said their lives were finally on the upswing."

Bee reported that Kelly had Face-timed her. He was working and studying hard as he would write some more exams in a couple of weeks. Grammy liked to hear that he was working hard.

"Grammy, Kelly said he missed you and your talks and good advice, not to mention the meals."

"Now, I want to show you a picture of Chelbee! Here she is. Isn't she so very cute?"

Carly explained to Dustin how Bee had assisted in Chelbee's birth at home. Chelbee was named after Bee and her friend Rachel who did the Cesarean.

There was another knock. Everyone yelled, "Come on in Mac." She asked how in the world they knew it was her?

"There was one person missing so we hoped it was you Mac," said Dad.

How did Dad come up with that stuff? It was perfect and Mac took a chair beside Mark.

They explained how Barry was Mac's Dad and how he found Andy's sister Bella. At this point Dustin was totally confused but was amazed at just how many lives this family was intertwined with. He found it difficult to follow all the conversations going on at one time and thought it was his language barrier. We could have told him it was not going to get any better. Grammpy was trying some of the old Amish German on Dustin and he was able to understand many words similar to his German. What luck that he found a family with German heritage that understood his background and language even somewhat.

Dad was taking Dustin out in the morning and they would stop at a few places. He would be home shortly after lunch. They would stop at a subdivision so he could have a look at how the work was done in Canada. He and his brother expected that they would have to get some on the job experience and then write an exam after they knew the codes. It was a matter of finding a company that was willing to give them a chance to learn.

Angela called the next day to talk to Mom. She wanted to say that

Dustin and his family could stay at her house until they got settled. It didn't matter how long it took. Mom was speechless. Mark had told Angela about them and how they wanted to come to Canada and make a fresh start. She wanted to give back and this was an easy way to do it. Mom told her it would be up to Dustin and his family and she would send him over later to have a look at the house.

Carly came over to see Bee and Dustin in the afternoon and they went over to Angela's before going sightseeing. Angela had four bedrooms and a den they could use. The boys could share a bedroom and their mother would have her own place to sleep. Dustin was amazed how large the coach house was and said it had more room than their modest home in Germany. Angela told him she was glad to share what she had and they would be welcome. They agreed, it was perfect.

The rest of the day was spent in Niagara Falls, going on the Maid of the Mist, walking Clifton Hill and watching the Imax Theater. Dustin had seen some of the information shown in Germany and wanted to see more. It was interesting how he and Carly managed to end up sitting together most of the time. Carly was an energetic person with a twinkle in her large brown eyes. Her hair was curly one day and straight the next, depending on her mood, or the occasion. She loved to dress well, putting thought into her wardrobe. She always looked smart even in a pair of old jeans and tee shirt. Bee had experienced so many good times working with her and they had become very close friends.

After a few days, it became normal for Carly and Dustin to make their own plans. No one minded this quickly blooming relationship. They seemed so right for each other. You could tell they were both head over heels for each other. Bee watched Carly and wondered if "she" acted as goofy around Kelly. When she asked Josh that question, he suggested she was worse! That of course was a brother's point of view.

Dustin lined up a job possibility for Mitchell and himself. He knew they had a lot to learn as the German buildings were not built of wood and they rarely had air conditioning. It would take some work. They could do it, having the new opportunity of living in Canada. Their mother would enjoy this property and the fellowship of the people around her. They would have an income every month from the museum and it would get them started. He would leave for Germany in four days. Carly was going to miss him as much as he missed her.

It was a special evening as Mac and Mark had been invited for dinner. This was strange as no one else like Dustin or Carly or Grammy and Grammpy were invited. Dustin was out with Carly on their last date before he left for Germany tomorrow.

Josh suspected that they were in trouble and his parents had discovered one of the trio's secrets. That had to be the reason for the closed meeting. They nervously sat down and waited for the bomb to drop. Josh figured they must know about him falling off the cliff.

No one said anything and Josh finally said, "Dad, what is going on?"

Mark and Mac just looked on with fright in their eyes. Dad said he had a surprise and they could go on a trip to South America!

"Oh I thought you found out about the time I fell off of the cliff!" Josh blurted out in relief.

Mom jumped to her feet and said, "You what?"

Josh could not believe what a blunder he had made. He just forgot for one second. He told them all about that terrible day in the rain and continued with the fact that they were all safe. After listening to warnings that seemed to go on forever, Josh thought he would try to change the subject. It was all he could do to sit there and listen to the same thing over and over. He agreed that he deserved every bit of the lecturing. After all, it was his own slip of the tongue that brought this on.

"What were you telling us Dad, you know, about some kind of trip?"

Dad caught his breath and reported that yes... he was going to tell them they were going to South America, to try to find the Kempt family.

"What do you mean? We can still go, can't we?" Josh insisted.

Dad acknowledged yes, they could go. The three all jumped for joy. Dad would pay for it, as it would come out of his inheritance from his ancestor. Mac and Mark were stunned. They would need to get their family's permission and couldn't wait.

Dad informed that Rudy Kempt left his money to the soldier Herman Wolfgang, who helped the men while in the tunnels. The Wolfgang family moved to South America. Eckhart Kempt's family was also located in South America, but were not sure in what area yet.

"Do you kids have passports?" Dad asked.

"I do," said Mac.

"When did you want to go?" questioned Mark.

"As soon as possible."

We were all in an uproar except for Bee, who looked a little disjointed. She expressed that she would rather stay here, as Kelly was coming every weekend for the next three weeks. She wanted to see him. Dad understood young love as he had been young once himself. He let her know that she would be missed, but it was her decision. Mom was staying home too and it was Pa, Dad and the three rascals. Mom and Dad started on the fact that Josh could have gotten killed when Grammpy came in and wanted to talk to Dad privately. He excused himself and with a puzzled look left for the new addition. Everybody wondered what that was about.

CHAPTER 15

The Proposal

As Dad sat and made himself comfortable, he noticed Grammpy had disappeared. Suddenly, in front of him, stood Kelly. He looked nervous. Dad asked if anything was wrong and of course he said no, on the contrary. He expressed his love for Bee, which Dad knew, and he would like to ask permission to marry her. Dad announced he was not ready for that yet! Kelly made known that he wanted to get engaged and marry next summer.

"You know, I think you are the right man for Bee and I give you my permission to marry her. I will have a year to get used to the idea. Thank you for giving me the privilege to say yes."

Grammy and Grammpy came back into the room and congratulated Kelly for his courage.

Dad asked, "Is this supposed to happen so soon?"

"Since it involves you and your house I will let you know," said Kelly. "Tonight I will climb a ladder up to Bee's bedroom and knock on her window. Hopefully she opens it for me to climb in so I can propose." Grammy was ecstatic.

"Do you have a tall ladder?" asked Dad.

"Yes, it is already there!" Kelly replied.

"Well, I will go back home and pretend this never happened," Dad sighed.

Dad went back just as the door was opening and in came Carly and Dustin. They had a nice evening together. Dustin asked what the ladder was for and Dad covered by saying he was checking the eaves and found he would have to do some repairs.

"Did it get in your way?" Dad asked considerately.

"Oh, no," they replied, "we just wondered, and is Kelly here and did he have car trouble?"

Everybody looked stunned but Dad asked, "Why?"

Apparently there was a car down the road that looked like his. Dad suggested it could be someone else's.

"I wish he was," said Bee sadly.

Everyone sat around and chatted all evening. Mac and Mark finally went home, Josh went to bed and Dad suggested Bee turn in too. She looked rather annoyed with her dad, as she was old enough to stay up all night if she felt she wanted to. Dad said good-night and so did Mom and they turned in. After a while, Bee felt like a third wheel and decided to leave Dustin and Carly alone. As soon as she went to her room Dad sent a text.

"Who are you texting?" Nerissa asked.

Dad said he would tell her later. Dad seemed nervous and Mom couldn't figure out what was happening.

"Are Grammy and Grammpy all right?" She quizzed.

He tried to focus on a TV show and tried to look relaxed. He wondered what was happening. Hopefully the ladder wouldn't slip. Suddenly there was yelling.

"Mom, Dad, look!" Bee shouted.

Everyone was out of their bedrooms and wondering what was going on. There behind her, was Kelly...in her bedroom...?

She was waving her hand.

"Look, I am engaged," she proclaimed. Mom hugged her and then examined her ring. Then Dad, then Josh, then Pa. Of course Kelly was congratulated too and welcomed to the family.

"Is everything all right up there?" came a shout from Carly at the bottom of the stairs.

Bee ran downstairs and everyone followed. Grammy and Grammpy were waiting for them.

"Look Grammy. Look Grammpy. I am engaged," she shouted hugging them.

Carly looked shocked, "You are engaged? Let me see the proof!" She grabbed Bee's hand and jumped up and down. "I am so excited for you. How awesome! Can I be a bridesmaid?"

Bee had to stop. She went over to the man of her dreams, Kelly and gave him a big hug. She wondered how he got there and when. How could he afford such a beautiful ring? Did he go through the proper protocol and ask her Dad?

They all sat down to find out details. Carly was so glad to be in on this life changing moment. Grammy and Grammpy knew for some time. Grammy had no use for the family diamond ring that had been passed down to her from her grandmother. Since she agreed to live in the Amish community this kind of jewelry would not have suited her. It was waiting for her granddaughter. She offered it to Kelly when he confided that he wanted to marry Bee. Grammy was honored that he appreciated and accepted the family heirloom as an engagement ring.

Bee said again, looking at her ring, "It is so beautiful Grammy. Who owned it first? I never knew you had it Grammy!"

"It belonged to your great, great grandmother. They were very well to do when they left Germany for their new land of freedom. Being wealthy was not as important as having your religious freedom," Grammy continued.

Bee hugged Grammy once more and assured her she would appreciate the ring and the story for the rest of her life. She felt so blessed to have such a rich legacy to draw from. They all sat around talking and filling in the blanks until suddenly they realized it was very late. Bee asked Carly to sleep over and she texted her parents to let them know. Dustin would leave for the airport tomorrow. Everyone was tired and went to their rooms to get some sleep. Kelly bunked up with Josh again. I guess this was going to be his brother-in-law, and that's what brothers do. Bee had talked to Mom about the family secrets, and Mom said she could tell Kelly if she was sure he could keep a secret. Sometimes you don't tell people because you want to make it easy for them. Bee knew he wanted her safe and knew he would handle it just fine.

The morning came quickly. Mac and Mark returned early in the morning to report that they were being able to go to South America.

They got a huge surprise when Kelly sat at the table and Bee was grinning from ear to ear.

Mac noticed instantly and shouted, "You're engaged!"

She studied Bee's diamond like girls do and exclaimed, "Oohlala! How much did this break the bank for? She didn't really want to know the price, but was saying it looked expensive. Bee told the story and they were impressed. It sounded so romantic getting a tap on the window and then asking for your hand in marriage!

"Kelly, you sure started out well. How are you ever going to top that surprise?" Mark laughed.

"Well kids, what did your parents say?" Dad asked.

They said, "Yes," was the answer from both of them. We both have our passports.

"My mother has this thing about being able to travel to another country at a moment's notice, even though we don't have the money to do so," Mark announced.

"Worked well this time, eh Buddy," laughed Josh.

Mom inquired, "When are you going, now that all of you have passports?"

"If we can get flights out, it will be in a couple of days. Tell your parents we will be away at least a week or two. What did they say about the trip being paid? You didn't tell them where the money was coming from, did you?" Dad questioned, knowing he would wonder where the money was coming from if someone offered to pay for his kid's trip.

They shouted, "No," and they were off again, as they had so much to take care of.

Dad yelled after them, "Pack light!"

He didn't think they heard him and wondered if it mattered. The kids would pack what they wanted anyway.

"Well, I guess we have a wedding to plan while our men are away," Mom suggested.

"That will be fun," agreed Bee.

They decided to let the guys get on their way before they discussed the wedding. Bee took the weekend to discuss a few things with Kelly.

She told him of the secrets they held dear regarding this property. Kelly was so intrigued, that he decided to do his online studies from Bee's place. The story seemed so real and yet so impossible. He couldn't believe that Josh and Mac found this by accident without Pa and that Pa knew for some time and never told anyone. The story of Omz bothered him and the fact that Bee was almost purposely killed brought the danger close to his heart. After his studies, Bee was going to take him down to the tunnels. They invited Mom to come along, but she had some shopping and banking to do with Grammy. Kelly and Bee entered through the house entrance and Pa's study. The downstairs living quarters was exceptional, and he asked so many questions. They went to the storage room and down the stairs to the dark cavern. Bee was so excited to show Kelly everything. She forgot that they could have company. Suddenly, from nowhere, a cougar appeared. Kelly pulled Bee back. Bee looked closely and could see another in the background. In fact, she saw two pairs of eyes staring at her from the dark.

"Girl, it's okay Girl! It's me. I have a friend with me," she said, slipping Kelly a treat for Girl.

"Let her sniff you and she will be your friend."

"Are you sure?" He said hesitantly.

Girl came and got his scent. She sniffed the hand with the treat and he opened it. Girl enjoyed the treat and the two young ones came out of hiding. Bee sat down to play with them and pet them. Halfpint had grown a little and gotten much stronger. Sweetheart still loved Bee and wouldn't leave her side. They both got snacks. Kelly was still in a non-committal mode and Bee reminded him of all the stories she had told him. They were true and he could trust Girl. He started to pet Girl and Sweetheart. They thought he had a treat, so Sweetheart jumped on him. He just about died and couldn't believe this was happening. Bee had a chance to hold Halfpint and cuddle her. It was as if Halfpint remembered her. She snuggled right up to her face like she did in the sleeping bag. Girl moved and the young ones took note. They were ready to follow the parent again. Halfpint looked back at Bee as if she didn't want to leave. Girl made a noise and Halfpint was off and running. Kelly was still in shock.

"No wonder you love this place. It has beauty that no other place on earth has," he said.

"It is different than anything I have ever experienced," Bee agreed.

She told him about the other tunnels, the lake tunnel, the tomb tunnel, the tunnel with the soldier's skeleton, the tunnel to the electric plant and the dynamite. She continued as they went back up the stairs, coming out from under the gazebo. They returned going back down the stairs through the storage room. They sat and Bee answered all the questions she could. She filled him in on the gold and coins. They were working to give back to the ancestral families their rightful share. Kelly couldn't believe the story of Dustin and Mitchell's home and what Dad and Mom had found there. It was all too much for him. He would have to digest it all and put it in order in his head. Bee reminded him that her family lived every experience as it happened and he would put it all together too, in time. She iterated the fact that they never knew if there would be another Vinnie, hungry for money, and they had to keep this place a secret if they wanted to live here. He understood totally, especially since her life had already been put into danger. The good thing was that Mom and Dad had met some of the ancestors and built a relationship with them. They gained the once stranger's trust, and these people will believe it when Dad gives them the money equally divided up. The last thing we want is for someone to think we are keeping their money. Kelly understood totally what she was saying. He wanted to see more and hear more, but for now they would have to go back. She showed him where to sign in and out. It was the rule. He also had to understand that Grammy and Grammpy did not know. It was up to Mom and Dad to let them know when the time was right. Kelly could not believe the magnitude of this secret and how it could change so many lives. There was the overwhelming sadness of the prisoners, who were sent to their death, after working to create these tunnels.

"How is this cruelty possible. How can mankind do these things to one another?" Kelly questioned.

Bee asked herself the same questions many times. She herself came up with no answers, except greed, dominance and hate. She thought she could never want someone dead until they tried to kill her. Her fear drove her to hate and wanted the person responsible punished and even dead. There was no forgiveness in her and she knew that it was wrong. She had learned through her near death experience that when people lost sight of what was important in eternity, they become irrational and different people. She knew God helped her to forgive Vinnie and his friend, as well as overcoming her fears.

"That is a heavy topic to end the day," Kelly acknowledged.

He admitted to be glad that they do not have to make any of those heavy hard decisions today. Today I love everybody, especially you, and I feel so good that I will have you for a wife. He kissed Bee with the passion that he felt and they went up into the living room of the old mansion.

CHAPTER 16

The Favelas

They arrived at their hotel. Dad, Pa and the three musketeers had a good night's sleep after the long flight from Canada to Rio de Janeiro. Mac flung the curtains open and we all protested, half asleep, with our hands over our eyes. There, with all the greatness that something man made could attain, stood the Christ the Redeemer statue, towering high above the city. We felt like it was watching over us.

Mac marveled, "Look! It is the Christ the Redeemer statue! It is so close."

We glanced towards the window and there it stood, bold, large and magnificent. It certainly was a wonder to behold. We were entranced by its size and the fact that we were here in person.

Dad had an appointment this morning to meet at the Institute of Land and Cartography and do some research. He and Pa would try to make it quick, knowing the teens would be itching to get out of the hotel and into the city. We had our cell phones and would be in touch to meet up later on. Dad and Pa both warned us to stay together.

The research proved to be interesting as it had been only a few years since the government gave people from the *favelas*, (slums) titles to their properties. They did this in entitlement by the communities, to try to fast track the process. To our advantage, this had happened only a few years before and would enable Dad and Pa to look for names. This was the last area that a descendant of the soldier, Herman Wolfgang lived.

Pa traced the family of Herman Wolfgang from Germany to South America. Our family was trying to locate the soldier that disappeared in action. They were aware that many soldiers had been secretly sent to South America during Hitler's reign and assumed he was one of them. Apparently, a letter to a cousin in Germany stated that Mrs. Wolfgang had no luck in finding her husband in South America, but decided to stay there with her children. The letter gave the vague address named the *"Favela"* and they had sent a photo of their home, as well as an old photo of their view overlooking the slum, with the ocean as a backdrop. It would have been impossible, as well as too dangerous, to find until now. The police were sent in to clean up the area, where violent gun wars happened daily. This was to free the area owned and run by the drug gangs. Dad and Pa learned about the newly painted sections of the *favela*, which sat right in between two of the most expensive zip codes in Rio. The painting of the buildings had made a difference in how the area looked as well as how the people felt about it. Giving the poor homes a face lift also gave the people pride. A chain reaction of respectful ownership was developing in the slums. Pa and Dad discovered so much in the research and with speaking to the manager of land transfers.

Dad was grateful the system had been updated and computerized. Pa was oblivious, as he kind of loved going through the old books one page at a time. The name Wolfgang showed up and they had an address to follow up. The owners had been granted the title of ownership and deeds to the properties recently. Talk about good timing! They were told that the houses did not have numbers or names on them yet. The house would be difficult to locate.

Meanwhile, the boys and Mac were walking the famous, "Ipanema Beach" when someone called out to them, "Hey *Americano*." It was early and there weren't too many people on the beach yet.

"Hey *Americano*," the voice sounded again.

They turned around to see a single figure leaning on a palm tree. He was noticeable even though he was beside the walkway. The design of the sidewalk demanded your focus with its black and white bold wave pattern. We acknowledged the stranger by nodding a hello. Mark even tipped the front of his baseball cap.

'That was nicely done," said Mac.

"Stop making fun of me."

"I wasn't," she rebutted. "It looked gentlemanly."

Suddenly there was someone right behind them, almost stepping on their heels. It startled them and they jumped aside. The stranger stopped and said he wanted to walk with them. They asked what he wanted and he said he just wanted to get to know the Canadians.

"You called us *Americano*, and now you changed your mind?" Josh asked.

"Yes, I have heard your accent."

He had dark hair and olive colored skin with a lean frame. He was very bold in quickly putting his arm over Mac's shoulders. Both guys, Mark and Josh, were astounded and were ready to tell him off. Mac took charge and flung the arm off of her shoulders and asked if he would please ask for permission to touch her. In Canada we did not touch strangers that way. The boys were shocked at Mac's courage. They always knew she had it in her. They just never saw this side of her in action before. She was direct, persuasive and in charge. Josh caught Mac's eye and gave her a wink of approval. She smirked back.

"What are you doing out here so early?" Clearly, most people were still sleeping. He asked us the same question, being evasive, but we said "you first." We Canadians felt he was a little shady so we were prepared not to believe him.

He lived up there, pointing to the brightly colored section, only behind it. It looked lovely from our vantage point and the view from there would be outstanding.

Mac asked, "Is it nice in your part of town?

He thought a moment and said, "You would not like it. You have wide streets and single family dwellings with hydro electricity, running water, sewers, many bathrooms in your homes with toilets that flush, properties that would fit many condominiums, roads for your cars, two televisions, large refrigerators, air conditioning and you have huge beds for only one person, with matching duvet sets!"

We wondered where all that came from. It sounded like he made an on-site study on the living conditions of Canadians and resented us for the way we lived. We let his answer be his opinion and asked again what his part of town was like. He said he hoped we would never see or experience it.

"What do you mean?" asked Mac.

He seemed to like Mac, so he could not resist but give her an honest answer.

"My home is a shack! Very narrow sidewalks and winding stairs lead to it. My front door is old and chipped and repaired with strips of tape to hold it together. My Father found an old door lock and installed it for a sense of security. The window beside the door is only half there. One side is better than none. It has bars coming from the top half of the opening. Our clothes are hung on lines strung under the window. Lola does not have to leave the house to hang the clothes up. She reaches out of the window to hang the laundry, as that is safer. The outside is very rough cement, making it look, in your language, "rustic." When you come into the small house, there is a very small front room with a television. We sit on the floor on blankets or boxes. The kitchen has an old chipped counter with a small under-counter fridge and hot plate above it. The dishes sit on the counter, as there are no upper cupboards. We cannot use the space under the counter, as the rats will get into the house. The open sewer runs through the middle of and under the house. It is open except my grandfather put wood over top of it. The rats have eaten a hole in the wood under the sink and are coming through. The wood is getting, as you say, "rotten." We sleep in the upstairs rooms although it is hot. We have a lovely rooftop deck but it has been too dangerous to use because of the shootings between the police and drug gangs. My mother and father were killed six months ago while sitting up there. Every day they shoot. It would be a nice place and we used to grow vegetables and so on. You would call it a "patio garden."

We were taken back as we saw no emotion in him regarding the death of his parents. How was that possible? Who did he live with? He did say 'we' sleep upstairs.

"Wait a minute. Who do you live with?" asked Mac sympathetically.

"I live with my sister, Lauren, who's nick name is Lola, who I mentioned before and two brothers, Joel and Adam. Adam is now like my brother. We found him and took him in."

We wondered how they found Adam? Did he get lost and they found him? How did they survive without parents? Maybe the other siblings were much older? We asked all these questions and got answers. Adam was a boy they took in a couple of years ago. He was found hiding behind their garbage bin after the shooting started. The teen told us his mother grabbed Adam and pulled him into their humble home. Adam had nowhere to go so he stayed. They had saved his life and would try to give him all he needed to become an honorable young man. Their father promised that one day they would all live in a better home. So far, they never made it.

We were overcome with sympathy until the young man said, "It is enough and I want to speak regarding other things."

"Well then how do you know so much about us?" Josh asked, not understanding how the new acquaintance felt.

"I study at the library and find out about you. One day I will go to Canada to make a new life."

"Do you go to school? questioned Mark.

"Not now, not since my parents were killed! I went to school until I finished my elementary school and then had to work. I attended from 7:15 until 11:45 am. In Brazil, they served lunch to 53 million children daily and I was one of them. The classrooms were 39 degrees Celsius with only one fan. It was very hot! I could hardly wait to go to work for three hours every afternoon and cool off. Afterwards, I would run to the cool air of the library and read about Canada."

"Why Canada?" Mac wanted to know. "Of all the places in the world it seems so odd for you to zero in on Canada?"

"My family have connections there."

"Really! Where do they live?" Josh asked.

"I am not sure." He answered.

Mac asked, "By the way, what is your name? We don't even know what to call you. I am Mac, this is Josh, and this is Mark."

She finished the formalities and he introduced himself as "Manny."

Josh said, "I know a Manny back home. He is Italian! I don't know what his full name is. Is that your full name?" Not waiting for an answer, he asked, "Do you think you can show us around your part of town, Manny?"

We wanted to see the area, as it sounded dangerous and interesting, like no place we had ever been to.

Manny did not want to expose us to danger so he said, "No. The government is promoting tourists to come to the *favelas* (slums) but not to my area. It is not safe yet. My family is hoping that one day it will be safe. Right now, my family is having a battle with a financier in Germany, who says the property is his. It has been in our family for generations and we know it is ours. Not only this home, but, one on a main street a little further down the hill from ours. We have to rent it out being the better building and is in a safer area of the neighborhood. People will not rent up where we live. My father put all his money into... as you say, upgrading. It has new floors, walls, cabinets, toilets, proper sewers, running water and electricity. I can show it to you sometime. You will like it. It is Canadian looking."

Just then the phone rang and we were shocked at how long we had been in conversation with Manny. We learned just a little about him, but he knew everything there was to know about Canada. He even knew what Ontario was like and that it was a province. He was a clever guy, that was for sure. He would be thrilled to know about our special place, the tunnels, but of course we could not mention them.

"Hi Dad, what's up?" Asked Josh.

"Pa and I are done, where should we meet? How about back at the hotel." Dad suggested.

After we agreed to meet Dad at the hotel restaurant, we needed to make arrangements with Manny to meet again. He suddenly left us and ran quickly, disappearing into the city scape. We were upset that we did not get his address and full name so we could meet again. Two men dressed like thugs neared. As they passed by, they looked suspiciously at us. We wondered what that was all about. It was a good thing that we were meeting Dad and Pa as they gave us a weird feeling.

Finishing our lunch, we felt all caught up on each other's morning. Dad said it was interesting hearing about the *favelas*, as that was the next place he was going to investigate the next morning. We made him promise that we could go too, and he agreed. We would spend the afternoon going up to the foot of the Christ the Redeemer, an iconic attraction, one of the seven new wonders of the world. After seeing this gigantic piece of art on television during the Olympics, it was going to be a dream come true. Later, we planned on taking the cable car ride with the "Sugar Loaf Mountain Cable Car," to see the awesome views.

The closer we got, the more monstrous the statue looked. We took pictures in front of its massive presence, realizing how small in comparison we looked. It was definitely an overwhelming moment. We had to pinch ourselves to the fact that we were there in person and experiencing this!

We were off to the aerial car. In the middle of the hustle and bustle of our journey to Sugar Loaf, Mark asked about the photo of his ancestor Joseph Schultz. The family had not taken the time to look at the photo to see if there were any hints as to which one was his skeletal remains. It must be on Mark's mind, as he mentioned it so often. Dad and Pa realized this would mean a lot to Mark and they would make it a priority when they got back. Dustin had left some old photos at the mansion so they could study them.

The mansion was getting to be a busy thorough fare. We loved every minute of it, but needed to remember that these very small tasks added up to be huge ones to people we loved, and it meant the world to them. We needed to harness our time and dedicate a portion of it to some of these tasks.

We soaked in the views of the cityscape and the ocean, taking in every momentous second from all angles. Our photos were going to bring back these feelings of awe. We just wanted to do it all over again, but the jet lag was catching up with us. We were feeling fuzzy headed and took a taxi back to the hotel. It would be a quick supper and we would call it a day. Mac loved her little nook away from the males in the group, who shared two queen size beds. They were all looking forward to a good night's rest.

Everyone got up and showered in no time in the morning. Breakfast was at a McDonalds around the corner. It was reasonable and quick. Our backpacks were ready for an adventure today. Josh even had his exploring pouch which Dad told him to put out of sight. It drew attention to itself and would be targeted for theft, as it appeared too interesting.

We took a cab up to the *favelas*. The cab driver warned us to be careful. Dad reminded everyone to stay together. The buildings were painted in varied solid color with waved lines of contrasting colors moving across many buildings. Before us stood a supersized mural painted three stories high. The four connected buildings made it look like one large canvas consisting of a happy, artistic collage portraying faces laughing, clapping hands and dancing feet. It brought joy to everyone who gazed upon it. We walked up a narrow set of stairs until we were at the back of these buildings. The happy feeling left quickly as the color turned to many shades of grey. It was old, dirty, gloomy and giving us the feeling of sadness. Color was definitely important. We saw for ourselves the mood change from bright color to grey. We were becoming anxious and fearful. Dad and Pa said they were looking for a certain place that overlooked the bay and the other homes.

"Dad, do you know how many shacks have that view?" Josh announced, as he looked at the copy of the photo.

"We were told how dangerous it is up here!" Exclaimed Mac.

"We should have a guide," added Mark.

Pa suggested that we ask the first person we meet to show us to the Wolfgang home. That is what we would do. As we climbed higher, we couldn't figure out where the people were. This place was full of thousands of people. Every stairway we climbed was empty. It was an eerie feeling. Dad reminded us to stay together, no matter what and be aware of our surroundings. We were on a very long narrow flight of cement stairs. They ran from the bottom of the *favelas* to the top, winding around the small shack like buildings. There were two men coming towards us in the distance. We would ask them. They neared quickly as we were climbing up towards them and we noticed they had guns in their belts. Something they held in their hands glimmered in the sun. They looked like they were going to cause problems. We took a turn onto a walkway in the opposite direction and hurried, turning many corners, hoping they would not follow. We could hear them and they were getting closer. Suddenly a door opened and someone grabbed Mac, who was closest to the building. They waved for us to come in and we hurried to hide from the men. The door immediately closed and we were led up the stairs. The man told us to hide in the closet. We passed a young woman frying something as we made our way through the downstairs quarters. The young man that waved us in was tall and slender with dark short hair and a narrow face. He had a contemplative look and relayed a look of danger to us. We got into the closet, but Pa looked for a better spot after the man left us there. He looked out of the window. There was a ledge that seemed to go around the corner and would hold all of us. He told us to get out of the closet and move around the corner. Dad went first onto the ledge and when he got around the corner, he found a shed-like structure big enough for all of us to hide in. Dad waved for us frantically. Pa was last and we heard yelling in the house. Pa made it around the corner, too. We could hear a woman screaming as she was pushed to the floor and a man yelling, "No no." The men ran upstairs searching for us. The closet was torn apart. Our hearts were beating so fast that we thought they would be able to hear them. The noise subsided and we heard them go to the next house. Our rescuer peeked out of the window looking for us, wondering where we went. Dad went back in to see if it was safe. It was, and we followed.

"How did you know to go out there?" the rescuer asked.

Pa said, "Someone told me this was not safe," pointing up to heaven.

"I know this Someone too," said the stranger.

We were delighted that he could speak English so well and ecstatic that he knew the Man upstairs too.

He asked, "What are you doing here?"

First of all, we apologized for putting his family in danger. We then told him we were looking for a family with a German origin called Wolfgang. Our rescuer became white and sat down on the bed.

"What do you want with them?" he asked with a voice of caution.

"We are doing research on the family and wanted to find them," Pa answered.

"What is the research for?" he prodded.

"It helps us to know why people immigrated after the war and where they went," Dad suggested.

Pa explained that we brought the young ones for a bit of a vacation. Our host was skittish and we didn't know if we would get answers. His sister came upstairs to see what was going on.

"Lauren, go back downstairs," he commanded, wanting to protect her.

Mac, Mark and I dropped our mouths.

"Are you Manny's Lola?" we whispered.

"Where is Manny?" Josh asked.

We were told again, by our hosts, to whisper. Somehow people heard what was said.

Mac looked up into her rescuer's compassionate eyes and quietly asked if he was Joel. Now we had them stumped and thinking. The brother and sister looked at each other and had no choice but to admit it was them. Dad made sure to repeat the fact that we did not mean to harm them. I asked if we could sit down and we did so. We sat on the four single beds with Lauren and Joel.

Dad believed God led us to their home. He, "God" verified it by the kids meeting each other the day before. That is a miracle in itself.

Josh interjected that Manny had said they were having problems with their deed, and a German financier wanted to take ownership of their properties.

"My Dad and Pa have been researching your name and the deed has been issued in your name a few months ago," he added.

"Why haven't we received it then?" Joel asked, more frustrated than ever.

"I do not know, but what I do know is that I can get you a copy at the same place where I saw the original one, with no problem," replied Dad.

Joel and Lauren looked relieved and a smile tried to make its way from the corner of Lauren's mouth. This was very good news. Joel asked what we wanted to know.

Dad asked if they knew why the family moved from Germany to South America. They answered that of course they knew that! Their great grandfather left a wife and a son in Germany and was forced to fight in the war for Hitler. He did not want to bear arms because of his faith, so they said they had a special job for him. He did not know what it was going to be. He was sent to South America and then we don't know what happened. We know this because he sent a letter to his wife in Germany, saying he was in Rio de Janeiro. He also described the property and sent a picture of the purchase. He sent his first paychecks from this address and then no one heard from him again. Our great grandmother traveled to Rio and then stayed here after looking for her husband. She expected him to come home and look for her when he was able. We have all the letters in our bank safety box. They are not safe here.

"We can see that!" Dad agreed.

My grandfather lived in the first house, this one and continued to do well in business. He bought the next one a few years later. My father upgraded the second purchase to its best potential as the area had been recaptured from the drug lords.

Joel anguished, "I don't know how long we can stay here. Manny is getting mixed up with the drug gangs! They want him to make money for them. He knows better, but is swayed because of their persistent threats to our lives.

"Hopefully we can do something for you when we get out. I do not think we will be up here again. It is too dangerous. Here is our address and phone number. You can come and see us at the hotel. I will need to see those letters from your great grandparents."

Suddenly there was a noise at the door and Manny came in. Staggering, he called to Lola from the main floor. He dragged himself up the stairs.

Lauren almost screamed and Joel grabbed Manny. He was beaten and bloody. His clothes were torn and he had cuts on them.

"Did they try to kill you?" Lauren asked.

She had a tall thin frame, but you could tell she could take charge of any situation.

Her long hair quickly pulled back into a pin-less bun, she went to work. She wanted to know if he was hurt. Did he do anything bad? Will they be back to finish him off? Joel said they would need to be ready. There was another noise at the door. Everyone froze. The youngest member of the family, Adam, entered. Being ten years old, he had been at school and then went to work.

"Lauren, where are you?" Adam called.

She called for him to come upstairs. He was shocked at all the strangers and most of all at Manny, who was hurt. One cut had made a gash across his chest. Dad said if Lauren sterilized the needle, he could stitch it for him. He hoped she had something to sterilize the wound and numb the pain. Everyone else was standing and Manny was now lying down. He said the gang wanted to kill him because he would not go after the five strangers in the *favelas*. He refused, especially as he recognized them. They were the friends he met just yesterday.

"I could not do it Joel; I could not do it!" he cried.

"That is good, Manny! You are a good boy! That is good!" Joel cried with him.

Adam stood there totally confused at all of this and had huge tears rolling down his cheeks. Mac went to him and held him tight. The group was feeling totally helpless, not knowing which way to turn. Poor Adam was letting out the full force of all his emotions. Pa said a prayer and asked for a miracle for this family as they didn't know what would happen next.

"Come over here," Mac said to Adam, taking his hand.

She led him to the corner of the room and sat down, pulling him beside her on the floor. She sat and held him as he felt comfort and love all rolled into one hug from this nice stranger. He stayed there until it was all over. We all wondered how Adam got back and forth to school and work without getting shot. The dangerous life here became so normal.

Manny was finished getting his stitches and crying that he was a bad person, just like his great grandfather who was in Hitler's army. There were many facts exposed regarding Hitler's army and the many cruel things they did here in South America. Manny linked those stories with his bloodline and figured he had inherited bad genes.

Mark jumped up to the plate. "I thought the same about myself. My relative was even more closely related. He tried to kill me and I got away. Only my body got away as my mind felt scared as to who I was. I figured maybe I had bad genes in me. No such thing, I was shown I am different just by what I do and what I don't do. You look at who you are. Manny, you did not go and find us to hurt us. You love your family and you are smart. Do you hear me?" he asked.

"Do you hear me?" He asked again, demanding an answer.

"Yes, I hear you, friend," Manny said with confidence.

"When you forget who you are, look at these people in your life!" Mark added.

With tears in her eyes, Lauren went downstairs to prepare some food to eat. They would eat on the floor upstairs, as downstairs was too unsafe.

Lauren came upstairs with some chicken, beef, potatoes and corn. With the tablecloth on the floor, it became a lovely picnic of sorts. She asked us to keep our voices down as she did not want us to be found. Some of us ate with spoons and some with forks. It didn't matter, as we enjoyed their humble and gracious hospitality. She probably used their weeks' ration of food. We quietly talked about when we should leave. We would feel a lot better when we were once again at our hotel. We would leave just before total darkness. At dark, everyone came out and the partying and violence began. The alleys were full of drinking, drugs and sex. Just before dark it would be difficult to be seen in the shadows and everyone would be eating their supper inside their safety zones. It was the safest time. Dad said he could call for a police escort, but it would cause a lot of shooting. We would try it the quiet way.

We asked if they would be safe here. Dad would send the police after this gang and asked them to send messages to the hotel to inform us of their situation. Lauren came upstairs and gave Mac her oversized sweater for the trip down. It concealed her beauty and the holes in it made her unnoticed. What a wonderful compassionate woman she was. She worked hard and yet managed to keep her skin and hair so beautiful, as well as her elegant mannerism. She was not only a sister, but a mother to the family. At her age she should be enjoying life and so should Joel. We knew their future was brighter but could not tell them yet. We just wanted to pick them out of this environment and place them into our safe world.

We were nervous to get going and said our good-byes. We were off and Joel accompanied us. He hurried us down some side walkways until we hit the brightly colored houses. We summoned a taxi to head to the hotel and we waved to Joel. Without wasting much time, he quickly headed back up the hill to his family and responsibility.

Getting back to our room, we went over the days' activities. We spoke of Joel and how he put his life and his family's on the line saving our lives. Lauren must have had a horrible life barricaded in her humble home, not even going outside to hang laundry. It was like she was in prison all day. At least the others got to school and work even though it meant putting their lives at risk to do so. We couldn't figure out what they did all evening. It wasn't comfortable.

Dad was going back to get a copy of their deeds for them in the morning. He would also visit the police station and see what he could do. We were told to stay out of trouble and check in with Pa, who would be at the hotel. Mac wondered if we could help the young family out with some money. She would take money out of her account and make sure they got it! Dad thought we should wait and see what happened and see what they needed most. We could have invited them for supper tonight if we could get a hold of them. When morning came, it would be another exciting day for the younger tourists. They would take a trip to the rainforest. For now, they would try to settle in and have some R and R time. (rest and relaxation) The kids took out a mini travel Scrabble game and focused on that until they got tired. Dad and Pa were reading their notes and making new ones.

CHAPTER 17

A Home Forever Changed

There was a loud rapid knock on the door first thing in the morning. We looked through the door viewer to see who it was. It was Manny looking tense! We quickly let him in.

"The police are raiding our neighborhood! We had to get out!" He said, out of breath.

"Where are the others?" Pa asked.

"They are around the corner at the ice machine," he replied, trying to catch his breath.

Dad immediately commanded, "Please, bring them in."

Manny waved and the three ran into the room looking behind them. Dad assured them that there was no danger here. We all wanted to know what happened. Dad was thoughtful enough to order juice and coffee with some Danish pastries. He would take everyone to breakfast when his guests felt ready.

"Tell us what happened," Pa suggested.

They began telling the details. Just as the sun rose, they were awakened with loud banging on the door. They thought it was the gang but it was the police. There was screaming and shooting. The police were raiding the neighborhood homes and knew by the look of us we were not gang members. They told us to get out and run and not come back until tonight. We sleep with our clothes on, always ready for danger, so we left at that moment. We almost got hit with bullets firing our way. The gang that was interfering with our lives was being targeted.

"Did you tell the police?" Joel questioned, with an intense look on his face.

"No, I was going to see them today!" Dad replied.

"Well, you will not have to do that now," added Lauren.

Mac looked at her and wondered how she could look so beautiful at this time in the morning with no makeup on. She took notice of Lauren's large hazel eyes and nicely shaped eyebrows. She could be a model, thought Mac. Everyone knew Mac was a natural beauty but Mac didn't think of herself in that way. It was what was so charming about her. She thought no less, or more of herself, but appreciated beauty when she saw it.

Joel was concerned and rather anxious! He wondered if they would have a home to go back to. He had become the most compassionate, responsible caregiver for his young age. Adam was drawn to Mac's side for a loving hug. He stayed there finding comfort in this new strange surrounding. With a familiar person by his side he felt safe and protected. They spoke again of the bullets and how terrified they were. We could understand that, especially since their parents got killed that way. We all realized the most extreme devastation that these shootouts caused. The police were trying their best, even with innocent casualties.

"Well, should we get something to eat?" Dad asked when he felt the time was right.

"Yes," said Adam, "I am hungry."

They all chuckled at children's honesty and made their way to the restaurant downstairs. Their guests wondered if they would be welcome there, and of course, we reassured them that they were our guests. That is all the hotel needed to know. We must have looked like a sorry bunch. None of us had showered as we were suddenly woken up that morning. Our hair was barely brushed and we wore our inner outerwear, meaning checked flannel pants and tee shirts. We ordered family style. Pancakes, sausage, bacon and eggs, hash browns, toast and fruit were our choice.

Dad gave thanks for the lovely new friends and prayed for their neighborhood and home. He blessed the food. We all ate like there would be no tomorrow. The conversation was uplifting and positive as hope for freedom from the gangs was acknowledged.

Dad questioned, "Where do you go to church?"

They replied that they were Catholic and went to a new faith Catholic church. Pa asked what they believed. They had made a new experience with God at a meeting on the street. There were so many people that changed their lives that they started a new congregation. They loved learning about the Bible and were given a small New Testament by the street people. They had to share it, but their English had gotten much better since they read the English Bible.

Dad asked if Joel wanted to come with him to the land transfer office to pick up the deed for himself. Joel was excited about that. He said they could go by the safety deposit box and he would get the letters that had been cherished as valuables by the family. Pa was going to stay at home base, right here in the hotel. They decided the younger group members would go on the Rainforest Tour. They asked Manny, Adam and Lauren to go too, and this qualified the group to travel with a van. It would make for an enjoyable and safe trip.

Adam, of course, jumped for joy, "I have never been to the rainforest!"

We couldn't believe that. How sad. Mark reminded us of how some inhabitants of the Niagara area never visited the Falls in all its splendor. We agreed and wondered why you wouldn't take advantage of such an awesome experience in your own area. We, of course, realized that this family did not have the finances to take these luxury trips. This would make the day even more exciting. Dad made a call to change our reservations to six people and the company confirmed that we qualified and would travel in a private van. They would pick us up in an hour. We hurried to get ready. You can imagine, sharing one bathroom was not what us Canadians were used to. Dad wanted to give Josh some money to treat the rest for lunch or water if they needed it.

"No Dad, I was going to use my spending money to treat them!" he protested.

"That is unselfish of you Josh, and it will be a blessing to you too," Dad affirmed.

Josh sensed that Dad was proud of him and he felt so good to be continually affirmed and built up. Who would he be if Dad were not part of his life? Who would he depend on for his confidence? As soon as he thought it, the answer came to mind. He knew he would get all he needed from God. This was the first time that this realization had been entertained by Josh. It was freeing. Even if no one was around he would be the person he was today, as he would never be alone. It gave him joy and put a spring to his steps. Mac noticed and asked what was making him so happy. He confided in her and she totally understood. That was the great thing about Mac; even though she was a girl she understood what he was talking about.

CHAPTER 18

The Rainforest

The shuttle arrived and they were off to see the rainforest. The plan was to take the "Tree Canopy Tour" once they reached their first stop. They wondered if Adam would be too terrified to try it.

He participated and was willing to do anything. He did not show that he knew the meaning of fear! He stepped onto a rope with a log attached every foot or so. You would have to hang on tightly to the ropes at the top for balance. Of course, you were harnessed. It was quite a job keeping your balance and moving forward to cross the bridge. What a great job Adam did. Josh looked at him and his bravery. Adam would use it to display how grateful he was to have this special chance at life with a family that loved him. Along the way, they saw many monkeys. The walk through the rainforest made them cautious, as they spotted a large Boa Constrictor, only after it was pointed out to them by the tour guide. It was the same coloring as its surroundings, black with large brownish irregular circles on it. It blended so well with the log it was on that they would have missed it. They happened upon a Southern Coatis with its young. Although they were adorable and Mac wanted to touch them, we were given strict orders not to. Of course, we knew these animals were wild and it would be dangerous. Lauren loved the sloth as it lounged on the ground. It was the perfect reflection of its name. It was an awesome day enjoying each other and the fabulous and unique surroundings.

When we got back, Dad and Joel and Pa were looking at the letter.

There it was in black and white, that this family was the descendent of Herman Wolfgang. It was in Herman's wife's handwriting. Dad made copies of the letters and put them in a folder. The family would be inheriting the money from Rudy Kempt as directed in Rudy's will.

They watched the news in their hotel room as Pa had seen a clip showing the gunfire and innocent people laying on the ground injured. The gang members fought to the end and were all killed, as they did not know the meaning of surrender. The homes were all searched and many weapons were seized. Lauren, Joel, Manny and Adam jumped for joy and couldn't stop celebrating. We celebrated with them. We all decided to go with them to check on their home while it was still daylight.

As we neared the bottom of the hill, we were amazed at the noise. The atmosphere had totally changed. Although the area was a mess as far as damage to the homes, the people were dancing in the walkways and partying outdoors. It looked like the neighborhood had finally been liberated. When we got to the Wolfgang's home, we saw it was heavily shot up. The door was broken and there were bullet holes on the inside. The building stood adjacent to the hillside, or so they thought. Now that the back wall was damaged and opened, we could see that there was a room in between the house and the hillside.

"How was this possible?" Joel cried out.

They were not aware of this room. Josh grabbed his flashlight from his hidden out of sight pouch. He was so glad he had brought it with him this time. He went into the room with everyone following behind him. The light revealed bullet holes everywhere. You could see blood where the gang members had been shot. There were cases that looked like they had been full of weapons. They had been stored here, along with drugs. How did the family miss this? The inside wall of this room was heavily insulated, as was the ceiling. They were in shock at their findings. It was no wonder the police suddenly wanted them out of their home. This had to be the result of quite some investigation. There was a make-shift door at the back facing the hillside. We took the boards away and had a look. There was a ladder going from the second floor, down the back of the house to this opening.

"I think this is now part of your property, Joel. You have the deed that says it goes into the hillside, but how far into the hillside?" Dad rubbed his chin.

Lauren, still in shock spoke, "It is a good thing they were not here when you were hiding, or were they? It is such a scary thought!"

Joel announced, "I have to see if there is a room upstairs."

As he ran up the stairs, we all followed him. He took his foot and kicked a hole in the back wall. It was hollow. He made a bigger hole with his hands and Dad helped him. The flashlight revealed another huge room. How was this possible? They were able to get inside. The ladder came from the roof down to this level against the inside wall. It exited near the rock wall on the opposite side of the room.

"Let's go to the roof!" Joel commanded with excitement.

It was sunny and cozy, although all its contents were strewn everywhere. The markings from their parents' death lingered as blood was dried on the chairs where they sat when shot. Adam began to cry at the memory of that terrible evening. Lauren comforted him telling him it was going to be alright. They would have a better life now and he would be able to play safely up here. This was a magnificent spot to watch the sunrise and sunset, as well as feel the evening breezes. We noticed that the rooftop patio was built right against the rock face of the hillside. There was a very small space to climb down into the room below.

Pa suggested that the parents were killed because they saw more than they should have or to frighten everyone to stay off the roof so the gang members could access their stash at will. We wondered how they got to this point, as the rock wall was steep above them. Dad figured they climbed on the shed roof, which lined up with the floor of the outdoor area. He looked closer and noticed a board from the shed roof to the neighboring house. Dad stepped onto the shed and pulled the boards back onto their roof. He figured the boards could be used for repairs. They were long, eight-foot planks. No one would jump that distance.

"This is probably why they wanted ownership of your property," reported Dad.

They had established an unnoticed, well-hidden den to hide themselves in, if they could get in whenever they needed to.

CHAPTER 19

Gain Through Death

"You have gained yourself a nice piece of real estate! My congratulations to you! Along with it, you have quite the story to tell," Dad said.

Lauren lamented, "She would rather have her parents back and give all this up for them."

Mac hugged her and said, "Those are my sentiments, too. These are things that cannot be changed but the future you face can. Live your life honoring your mother and father, making them proud of you."

Everyone agreed, and they went back downstairs. Dad suggested when they were ready, we could help them get started to rebuild their home. He could help to make plans for the reconstruction and also help them financially.

Joel walked over to the side wall and with all his might, punched a hole through it.

"We will let the light in and not hide anymore," he shouted, as the setting sun shone into the room for the first time.

We all walked over and peered out. What an awesome view you will have and the most beautiful sunsets over the water. The view was breathtaking. You could see the whole length of the beach and the waves lapping onto the wide shore line. Reflecting under the city lights, we agreed it was a mind-altering view and it would be the best most tranquil home in the area. Josh knew the young siblings had money coming and with it they could make any changes they wanted.

Josh was still contemplating what his Dad said about having ownership of the property going into the hill. He wondered why the deed said that. It could have said to the rock wall.

"Dad, can I take my flashlight and have a good look around?" Josh asked.

"I will join you while the others start the cleanup," Dad replied.

They searched the face of the rock wall starting with the upstairs. There was nothing on the top or second floor. Josh could not believe they found nothing and confided in his dad that he was looking for a tunnel or something like that. His dad thought his mind was getting a little too active but humored him just the same. Josh scanned the walls on the lower floor and found a section of the wall that had been closed in with rocks and mortar.

"Look Dad, look what I found!"

Just then, a voice came from behind and took them by surprise.

"Well will you look at that!" said Pa. "I think we will be needing some help, don't you?"

He called for the others to stop what they were doing and to come and help. They worked together taking orders from Dad. A couple of huge rocks were loosened and they were able to dislodge them. They fell out of their spot and rolled onto the ground. It left enough of an opening to see what was in behind. Josh was the first to lean into the opening with his upper body and flashlight.

"It looks like a cavern!" he declared.

Dad directed the removal of enough rocks to make a nice sized entry that they could walk through, one at a time. He determined that the rock inside the cavern was stable and seemed a natural part of the land formation. They all entered, investigating with a few flashlights. It looked bare except for a hole in the floor. Dad shone his flashlight down into the hole and he discovered another opening. The hole was plenty big for a ladder to reach the cavern floor below. Mark, Josh and Joel ran to retrieve the ladder that the gang had used to access the building. It didn't take them long and they were back carrying the rustic old relic.

Dad stood it up in the opening and it went down about nine feet. He climbed down first to check it out and told us to follow. We were excited at the fact that we had discovered a couple of new rooms and now we had discovered some caverns. A quick look around tipped us off to the fact that this was used in years gone by. There were very old crates, an old cot that looked like it had been through the war and a couple of old blankets. An old soiled pillow still held its position of prominence on the cot after all these years. It appeared as though someone slept here.

"Please don't touch or move anything," Pa warned.

"We need to get some pictures later," Dad said as the flashlight moved in close on the pillow. "I think we should get some DNA samples from this too."

"Look over here!" shouted Mac.

Joel beside her acknowledged the find to be interesting. It was a tunnel large enough to walk in comfortably two by two.

"Can we check it out, Dad?" Josh asked, with a trail of echoes agreeing with him.

Everyone wanted to find out where the tunnel led.

"I am hungry," said Adam.

Mac remembered a snack bar in her pocket and gave it to him.

"That will help you, right, buddy?" she asked.

"It sure will," he agreed as he chewed.

"I want to say no, but, as we have learned in the past, every tunnel must be explored," Dad said before asking if we all wanted to go. Everyone was in agreement.

Adam said, "I am scared."

"That's okay, I understand," Pa comforted.

"We will relax at home and wait for the others, okay?"

Adam was eager to leave the tunnel as it had been a straining day and he had not yet recovered from the shooting and the house being torn apart. It had to be unsettling for an adult, never mind for a child, to have to live through. Crowding back to his mind, came haunting memories of the day his mother and he were separated when she was killed in a gang war. Pa told Adam they would fix up his bed so he could go to sleep tonight. That made him feel good and he seemed to relax. Lauren, Joel and Manny hugged their little brother and said they would be back soon.

The three of them, as well as the rest of us, went on our way into the tunnel. It seemed to be an easy walk. We were careful that we didn't take the effortless walk for granted. After an hour at a good pace, we reached another cavern. In it were boxes that once held ammunition and gun powder. The labels were in German, just like the ones in our tunnels. We spotted a large automatic gun, set up ready to use. It had no ammunition. Proceeding through the cavern into the night air after fighting with some overgrown brush, we knew why this gun was here. It was a great lookout over the ocean. You could see for miles and the Germans would be able to protect themselves or flee with the evidence when they needed to.

"I'll bet your great grandfather was the guard for this property and that is why it was put in his name; to avoid suspicion," said Dad. "He might have just guarded the house so the Nazi's could do their spying from here."

"In that case, why would he accept this house from them?" asked Joel.

"War is not easy to explain. It has become an advantage for your family so many years later. Take it as a blessing, Joel, not a curse. God turns ugliness into things of beauty." Dad encouraged, patting him on the shoulder as Joel conceded to the thought.

Lauren was in awe of the serenity in this place. She seemed frozen as she stood there. The clear sky, fresh air and the peacefulness was overwhelming. It was something she longed for, not knowing how or where to find it. Suddenly she sank to her knees and sobbed. It had all been too much and now her emotions gave way. Mac went and sat beside her, holding her tightly. Lauren had to be strong for so long, now she finally felt like she could be free and vulnerable as she broke. She finally felt safe.

Joel, looking at Lauren, agreed, "God does use strange things to heal and renew our spirits."

When Lauren felt like she could continue, we decided to go back, as it would take some time. Adam would be waiting for us. It was a quiet walk back as everyone processed their own thoughts as to what the situation was so many years ago. On the way back we found a burlap sack. It was sticking out from under an empty ammunition crate.

Inside, carefully wrapped, were some papers. We took a look at the them and realized that these were the orders to abandon the house and lookout tunnels. It was accompanied with the orders for Herman Wolfgang to be moved to Canada to a top secret assignment. The payment for his previous guard duties was to be this house. Joel held the papers, knowing that his ancestor held them too. He and Lauren studied them as though they would reveal even more, the longer they did.

"I will take these and put them in a very safe place," said Lauren. "Mother told us that her grandfather was reported to have been sent to Canada, and now we know for sure. Maybe we can find out where he lived?"

Josh and his family felt guilty as they knew where he lived and where he died. It was too early to say anything just now. The time would come.

At the house, Adam and Pa had done a fine job putting things back in order in the bedroom. They even cleaned the upper patio so everyone could sit outside and enjoy the warm breeze as they chatted about their discoveries.

After Dad described the tunnel and the ammunition, Pa agreed that it seemed that it had been used by the Germans during the war and maybe afterwards. That would have to be investigated some more. Pa had researched the Nazi activity in South America, as there were many locations of occupation uncovered. They feel there are still more to be discovered throughout the country.

"Can I see it when it is daylight?" asked Adam.

The question caused a lot of chuckling as in the cave it was always dark.

"I won't be afraid tomorrow," Adam assured. "Not if I can carry my own flashlight!"

"You can have your own flashlight, Adam," Joel added.

"Wow! I am going to have fun!" The youngest member of the family's enthusiasm was contagious. "I will be brave like I was on the bridge in the tree tops. I was brave the same way when I last saw my mother."

Everyone sympathized with the young fellow and how he mustered up all that was in him to make it through his fearful times.

"Adam, I want you to know that you are becoming a better young man every time you make a brave decision," Dad coached.

We all agreed and became his cheering team.

Lauren remembered the papers and took them out. Pa looked at them and was in awe of not only the information but the fact that they were hidden there for so long. He caught himself thinking this and realized he had seen more than just a couple of papers in his very own tunnels at home in Niagara. They were also hidden for this long.

Hitler left his mark of destruction not only on countries and buildings, but certainly on the lives and spirit of more families than one could ever count. This small gathering of people on the roof top patio was proof of that fact, as everyone there had been affected in one way or another.

Manny had been very quiet. We were finally able to pull out what was bothering him.

"I just feel like such a weakling and fool," he said.

"Manny, you do not have to think about the past anymore. You just have to entertain the future and what lies ahead of you. Be who you choose to be, without the pressure from the gang and you will be the man your mother and father wanted you to be," Mark encouraged.

"I want to do just that," said Manny.

"Well, it is possible," affirmed Dad.

On the way downstairs, we noticed the beautiful sunset and our new friends hearts were filled with anticipation and thoughts of what this home was going to look like. Dad had a plan and was going to reveal it.

"Do you know you will have the same view from both new rooms? It will be so different."

"Too bad Nerissa is not here to organize this project," Dad said while his thoughts were with his wife.

Mark was uncommonly quiet and finally spoke. "Can the church do a missions trip over here to help this family? Look around. There are many more families that need help in this area. We could start with Joel's church as our point of connection."

"Mark, I am so proud of you. What a kind thought. Let's see if we can get that going," Dad added.

"My church would love to be the go-between on this project!"

Joel added.

"The first thing we will do is plan the bathrooms and get sewers put in. Then the team members can stay right on the job and get more done," Pa announced.

The Wolfgang family was so elated and couldn't stop hugging us. We moved through the house, talking about the future changes.

"Did we eat supper?" whispered the youngest, Adam.

Pa said it didn't really matter, if we did or didn't, if we were hungry, we should eat, but where should we go? They suggested a small place in the entrance to the *favelas*.

That is where we went to enjoy a couple of South American pizzas. We ordered fizzy drinks (pop) and enjoyed our time together. Joel ordered for all of us, only after we convinced him that we had enough money to pay for it. Sitting in the outdoor patio, we could hear the partying and rejoicing on the hillside. It was a new chapter for many families. The police were liberating one neighborhood at a time. They always had casualties amongst their officers and we couldn't help but acknowledge their sacrifice in our prayer before dinner.

Dad drew a quick house design. He was good at visualizing a place and so was Pa. They had stopped to buy a notebook, pencils with erasers and some food for our new friends. The neighborhood convenience store was on the way to the restaurant. It wasn't long before he had the first floor drawn.

The stairs would remain to the left upon entering the front door. As you walked straight ahead, you would see the small open concept, but efficient kitchen. It would have a full-size refrigerator and stove. An island would separate it from the sitting room. The sitting room would have a couch and comfortable chairs and a cabinet with a television above it. There would be a small fireplace for those unusual but occurring cool days or evenings. On the side of the house where the hole was created by Joel, would be large glass patio doors exiting onto a wraparound balcony from the front. A large iron gate would keep this balcony private and safe from the walkways. At the end of the balcony, at the back, where the shed is now, will be an outdoor spiral staircase leading to the second floor bedroom level. It will also be a continuation to the rooftop. On the first floor at the back, in their new space, there would be a full bathroom with a bedroom off of it with glass doors leading to the wrap-around balcony.

Lauren was so excited just to see and hear the preliminary plans. She wanted to hear about the upstairs. Dad continued and pulled out the next sheet of paper to draw the upstairs set of plans.

The stairs come up where I said and there will be a large glass door at the top to get out onto the second floor balcony. There is a sitting room with wall to wall windows upstairs, along the balcony. The full bathroom is at the back, right above the kitchen for easy plumbing. This area will also contain the laundry. There will be three bedrooms upstairs as well.

They were clapping with delight when Joel asked and broke the mood, "How are we going to afford this?"

Everyone's face got solemn. Dad explained he was making long term plans, but needed to know where the sewer lines should go and then the plumbing. The electrical would be standard. He said, when the time came, he could help them out with a loan. That was if they agreed to the plans.

"Oh, I forgot to tell you about the rooftop" he said.

The roof top will include the entrance to the stairs, a nice wall on the neighborhood side and glass rail on the water view side. He put an outdoor kitchen along the rock wall of the hill. It housed a grill, sink and small bar fridge. The tiled counter would be traditional with colorful tiles and shelves underneath. He drew a table and chairs as well as a seating area for relaxing.

"Of course, the loungers were facing the gorgeous one of a kind views," Dad announced.

"Joel and Lauren, we will not get you into financial difficulty. These are plans for you to accept or not. I will give you an approximate price. We would like to do the sewer system for you as well as the plumbing. That will be at our cost until you can pay it back some day. I also have in those plans a chance for you to make some money. You could rent out the bedrooms upstairs as guest rooms. You would be able to make good money doing that. You could have a pullout couch in the sitting room upstairs."

Their minds were working, expressing that the boys could stay downstairs in one room and Lauren could stay upstairs in the small bedroom by herself. They would have two rooms to use as guest rooms and another room with a pullout. Dad said that was a great idea and they should add a two-piece bathroom for Lauren, so she was private at night and could lock her door. It was settled. The income would offset the expenses very nicely. Lauren would have a job right here in her home and still be there for Adam. Everyone was in agreement that these were great preliminary plans, both for the house and for the family's income. Joel would be able to go to university and Manny could finish his schooling too.

We had a wonderful meal and enjoyed getting to know our dinner guests on a new level. The young family gladly carried the groceries we purchased for them up the hill to their primitive torn-apart home. They walked with hope in their steps as they disappeared up the walkway, turning every few steps to wave, putting their groceries down every time. We flagged a cab and headed for our hotel.

Dad was going to leave us at the hotel with Pa with no agenda but to help the Wolfgang family. He would get the kids to help tear down walls and get rid of the rubble. They would be kept busy as well as love the work. Pa knew how to organize jobs and get permits etcetera. He discovered most of the buildings in the slums had been done without permits. Pa wanted to be sure it was done well to measure up to the new conditions stipulated for this area. Pa and the kids would stay for a while and get the project going. They had no idea how many days their work would take.

CHAPTER 20

The Kempts

"I have researched all I can from here," said Dad.

Pa asked, "What is the latest?"

"Well, the Kempts left Paraguay, as they found there were more and more German soldiers in Chaco Paraguay.

Since the Germans had captured Eckhart Kempt, the family was afraid of the German soldiers. They did not know why Eckhart was arrested with his brother and saw no reason for it. The family discovered that there were strangers spying on the two men and had them followed, as well as having their homes watched. The police said they had no evidence of this and could do nothing until the law was broken. "This information was in a letter sent by mail to a friend," said Dad.

"Where did they go?" asked Pa.

"I found papers that showed the family departing for Africa on the "Independence."

They believed their life was in danger so they left on the first ship out. Dad discovered from the passenger list that Eckhart Kempt's wife and daughter traveled together. It would be a challenge finding this family. He would travel to Africa, but knew they did not keep documents like other countries.

Pa and the kids could stay another week and keep Nerissa posted on their progress. He would be in touch with her as usual. Apparently, the wedding plans were moving along well and the family was doing fine on all fronts. Kelly had decided to stay awhile and do his online studies at the mansion. Nerissa noticed how bonded he was with Grammy and Grammpy and he seemed to enjoy, as well as need, to check in with them. It was good to hear he was very dedicated to the elderly couple as well as his studies. Dad loved to hear that and passed this fact along to us more than once. Bee had shown Kelly around the tunnels and he was absolutely blown away with what he saw and experienced.

"He met Girl," was Bee's comment to Dad.

Dad missed seeing how the slum project was going as he had many meetings. They had hired men to pour new foundations after the sewer was put down and connected. The sewer from higher up the hill had to be rerouted, so the city decided this was a good time to do it. They renewed section by section as the neighborhoods were liberated. It saved the family a lot of money.

They made sure the cavern behind the home was accessible with an insulated door. They could use it for a cold room or for storage. The access to the tunnel was secured with a heavy metal door and locked. Of course, a ladder was kept in the cavern so they could go to that peaceful opening on the mountain overlooking the water. The house was perched on the hillside with a fabulous distant view of the beach and ocean, but in view of other homes. In contrast, the family's secret and safe hideaway would give them a private intimate place to call their own.

The hand cement mixer sat in front of the house with someone continuously working it, making cement. It was wheeled to where they needed it. Up this high, amongst the buildings with no roads, it was a tough build. The workers seemed to be used to this kind of labor and were happy to do it. Pa and the kids had framed the downstairs walls. It was all coming together nicely, transforming it into a lovely home. The kitchen was distinguishable, as its island was already built, taking a prominent place in the open concept room. They were going to make concrete counters for the home. Pa wanted to get the downstairs bedrooms finished and plastered so the family could sleep downstairs while they worked upstairs. When the renovations got going, they realized there was enough room for two bedrooms in the new section at the back, including the bathroom. The cupboards were going into the kitchen in a week even though the walls were not yet completed. The stove, fridge and microwave were also going to be added at that time. This week, a couple of men from Josh's church took time off from their vacation to help with the build. They heard about the need and didn't wait, catching the first plane out. They slept on the floors or wherever. The bathroom was out of commission but the neighbor was so impressed, he offered his humble toilet to the crew. It was rustic but a least it was a toilet. The neighbor hoped someday, the city would do his sewer line, too. The city worked from the top to the bottom to upgrade lines. Pa would get a crew to finish the walls in the kitchen and bathroom as well as set a toilet, sink and tub-shower combination. The men had already cut in and installed the doors to what would be the first-floor deck. All rooms were so bright and open feeling. The house already had a new feel of warmth and the second floor wasn't even touched.

Maybe Dad would get back here to see how the job was moving along when he finished his research in Africa. If not, the kids would document with photos. For now, he was still here for one more night. Dad invited the workers from church to shower at the hotel and have dinner with him. They had worked hard for days and hadn't even showered. The possibility that everyone would be using the new bathroom was soon becoming a reality. It would make life much easier at the renovation.

We said good-bye to Dad in the morning and assured him that we would keep him posted. He looked kind of lonely as he went off to Africa by himself. It was at least a twelve-hour flight with a couple of stops and layovers. Because of our project, we were glad not to be going, although we wondered what Africa would be like. He had called Mom, Grammy and Grammpy and gave them his itinerary. He did not know what he would find until he would get there.

CHAPTER 21

Africa

Dad flew into Nairobi. He made it this far and needed some sleep. He knew a couple that lived in Africa and they agreed to pick him up and let him get his bearings for a couple of days. They could direct him where to start his research. They met where Dad was directed to wait for them. When Dad got into the van, he almost fell asleep. Rob said he had another pick up and Dad was okay with that. He could already feel the bed beneath him and knew it would be only a little while longer. Rob went to stop at another spot at the airport and got out. Dad closed his eyes and was gone, fast asleep. Someone quietly got into the van next to him and kissed him. He smiled as he thought he was dreaming. It was somehow familiar to him and he didn't want to wake up to see it wasn't Mom. Opening his eyes, he was shocked.

The story goes this way according to Dad's account.

"What are you doing?" he gasped in shock.

She had come to be with him and give him some support.

"Oh, Honey!" he said with gratitude in his eyes. "How did you get here? And why? Are Bee and Grammy and Grammpy alright?"

She looked at him with pity and said, "I felt sorry for you, Darlin', so I decided to come to see you."

Shawn quickly revived from his tired state of mind and embraced his thoughtful wife with one of his strong hugs. She also must have had a grueling trip!

Rob got into the front seat and asked, "Okay you two love birds, do you need something to eat?"

They both replied in unison, "No!"

Nerissa added, "No thank you, Rob, we are too tired."

Rob understood, of course, as he had made the trip too many times to count. His whole family had, but they loved Africa and their work kept drawing them back.

Nerissa and Shawn slept for a day and a night. Their minds were relaxed as they were together, together with the love of their lives. What could be better? Nerissa had some news for Shawn and couldn't bear to tell him on the phone from Canada. He had made such an effort to be here in Africa to research another name. They had a coffee and talked.

"Nerissa, what possessed you to come all this way?" he questioned.

"If you really want to know, I felt sorry for you. You were already in flight and I got the call to give you more information," she said.

"What information?" he wondered.

"The office that you dealt with in Paraguay called you in a panic. They needed to let you know something more regarding the research there. The man that you spoke with checked the records of the ship which the Kempt family sailed on, hoping that he would find an arrival date and port. Apparently, it sank during a storm in the Atlantic, on the way to Africa. There were no survivors recorded. No one was saved from the ship. He was sorry and hoped it did not inconvenience you. When I hung up the phone, I called you immediately but realized that you had already left. You told me when you would arrive so I synchronized my arrival with yours after calling Rob."

Shawn was in awe of how this woman loved him and was dedicated to him in every way. He couldn't believe it. It was an awesome surprise and lessened the blow.

"Thank you," he said appreciating that his words were not enough and sounded shallow in comparison to what he felt.

He kissed her, thanking her again for her outrageous effort.

"Well, at least you will have company when you fly back," she said.

"I don't think so, Nerissa," he frowned.

"Why?" she exclaimed, not understanding.

"We are going to take some time for each other, here, right now!"

he revealed.

"Here! Right Now?" she questioned.

Well, what Shawn meant was that they were not going home and would go on a safari first.

"I will get Rob to book one for us" he announced.

Nerissa was excited, as it was her first time to Africa. Shawn had been there once before on a mission trip. They spoke to Rob, who was going to take care of some matters at an orphanage called Pehucci. It was a great place for children to be safe from harm and get the provisions they needed to grow spiritually, physically and mentally. He would take them there first, to give Nerissa an overview of what the teams had done to help the community and orphanage. Nerissa would get to see this place she heard so much about. They would stay overnight at the orphanage and then head for the Maasai people. It was going to be the trip of a lifetime. Shawn reminded her that the safari would be after that.

They arrived at Pehucci later that day. The children were playing and having a good time. They looked happy. Nerissa wondered where these children would be without this orphanage. The lady who ran it had a great love for the children and they had such respect for Momma Lucy. Nerissa gave every child a candy. You could not give just one without the others having one too. Shawn showed her the building that they helped erect from the ground up and where the next project was going to be built.

They would treat the children to some fruit, purchased by the orphanage, but funded by them. It was a joy to see the children enjoying their mangos. The couple would be off in the morning. The roads were dusty and bumpy although Rob's vehicle was fairly new. Everywhere you looked were pictures to capture different customs, smiling faces and rustic markets at the side of the roads. Africa was unique and had an old-world charm.

The Maasai people were an exciting tribe, native to the land where they lived for generations. They were wealthy in cattle but lived simple lives. They were a colorful people and many of them loved God. We only stayed for a few hours and walked to the different buildings that our church had helped erect. Of course, we greeted many of the inhabitants of the village along the way. There were many mothers with babies and small children. Nerissa noticed so many flies on the children's faces and was tempted to swish them away. Rob explained that the people were very used to this and it didn't bother them. The cattle promoted the great number of flies. It was too much to imagine getting used to those flies, she thought.

"This has already been an amazing few days. Thank you, Rob," Nerissa said.

"You are welcome. I hope the next couple of days will leave you as thankful," he said.

Suddenly a cloud of dust went by them making it impossible to see. When visibility returned, they were beside a herd of zebras galloping alongside of their vehicle. Rob had to slam on his brakes to avoid some giraffes crossing their path. Nerissa screamed in fright and the men laughed. When she came to her senses, she started snapping photos. This was so awesome; never would she be so close to wild animals again, or so she thought.

Rob dropped them off at the safari and left to do his business with the Maasai people.

Nerissa wondered why they were out in the middle of nowhere and yet this was such a beautiful spot. The place had large tent structures that looked like homes on the inside. They had beds, furniture, closets, dressers, bathrooms and phones. It was unbelievable. The linens were snow white and so were the fluffy towels. The bathroom in their tent was luxurious. It was hard to believe. The bathroom was as modern as anything Nerissa had ever seen.

We will have breakfast in the morning and then go out on safari. Nerissa did not know what to expect. She was excited and yet nervous regarding their excursion. They had a good night's sleep and they woke early to enjoy breakfast. The safari vehicles were open jeeps to get the best views. Nerissa wondered if she would be safe, as the animals could also see them.

She got so close to the lions that she could smell the carcass they were tearing apart. She saw a wildebeest being chased down by a tiger and thought of Girl and could, or would... she, kill like that? The hippopotamuses were bathing in the river next to huge alligators. Her camera was working overtime capturing as much of the Maasai Mara as possible.

The rhinoceros was allusive and hard to find, but they did. She got some great shots of it before it tried to disappear behind some bushes. Nerissa and Shawn had the time of their lives. Back at the camp, a lovely meal was prepared for them and they enjoyed tasting the wild meats. On the way back to their tent, as it was just getting dark, everyone started to yell loudly and run. The commotion was loud and disturbing. They could not understand what they were saying. The shouts sounded scary and Shawn said they better get inside. While starting to run, they saw something coming down the road. It was a rhino!

Shawn knew these animals were vicious and killed more Africans than any other animal. He grabbed Nerissa's hand and pulled hard. They ran through the thick trees into a utility building where they hid. Heavy thumps of the rhino running nearby was heard. The rhino again moved on and ran down the road. The road ended at the river and every once in a while, the rhino would get lost and take a short cut through the compound to get to the water. There was a loud commotion of shouting as the men working for the camp came looking for their guests. They carried torches and flashlights as well as machetes and spears. They accompanied all the couples to their tents and Nerissa asked if they were safe in a tent.

"Yes, yes, Mum, you are safe!" they repeated over and over, slightly bowing with respect.

Nerissa wondered why everyone ran as they screamed if they were so safe.

The warrior told her, "This does not happen much, Mum. Only one time."

Supposedly safe in their tent, they had a hard time falling asleep. They talked for hours and finally drifted off. The next morning, they were going out before sunrise. It would be even scarier.

The jeeps were ready and waiting in the dark. They were off again. They didn't know what they were in for this morning. The jeep ride in the dark was relaxing until they caught sight of some eyes glaring like lights and watching them. The sun started to rise on the horizon and all was forgotten. There was an air balloon rising in the sky and many ostriches running across the horizon beneath it. With the sun rising as a backdrop, it was a most magnificent picture. Then, Nerissa noticed a single tree in the distance and captured another perfect shot. If they saw nothing else, it was enough. It was a memory that will stay in her mind forever, as a perfect morning. They went for breakfast upon their return and headed back to the tent to have an impromptu catnap. They slept until noon and it was time to eat again. You could hear the monkeys screeching in the trees. We decided to stay right there and enjoy the sounds of Africa. How amazing!

"I must say, I am starved," said Shawn as it was nearing dinnertime.

"I wonder why?" Nerissa chuckled. "We missed lunch you know!"

"Are you going to be long getting ready?" he asked with his stomach growling.

She took her hair and gave it a twist as she clipped it up. She was ready.

"That's what I love about you," he said while planting a, "thank you for being you" kiss on her. "You can look high maintenance and you can also be ready to go in a second. What a girl I married."

The dinner was once again outstanding. Nerissa was nervous about walking back to their tent.

"When we hear loud yelling we will move," Shawn sympathized.

He assured her that they would be fine. Tomorrow, Rob was picking them up early in the morning to take them to Nairobi. They would catch the plane home the next day and they still had to book their tickets. Shawn did not know how long this trip would keep him in Africa, so he had decided to book a one-way ticket. The kids and Pa had five more days to work in Rio. Nerissa wondered what the people were like there, as she had heard so much about this young family.

"Would you like to go there?" asked Shawn.

"Isn't it too much right now?" she asked.

"I don't think so. I will tell you what; if we can book tickets from here tonight, we will go!" Shawn was always ready to make a challenge out of things.

"We are living totally spontaneous lives, aren't we?" Nerissa laughed.

Shawn worked to book tickets online. It took him such a long time that Nerissa dozed off, although she wasn't even tired. Suddenly, she was wakened with a gentle quiet kiss, and when she opened her eyes a loud party tone yelled, "We are going to Rio!"

Shawn felt like he had defeated the world. It was a challenge, but he did it!

"When do we leave?" she asked, stunned.

"First thing in the morning. We can pack and not unpack when we get to Nairobi."

"That makes it easy!" she proclaimed.

It was going to be exciting and she would look forward to seeing Josh and Pa. She wondered if there was room at the hotel for them all. They would figure that out when they got there.

Rob couldn't believe about the rhino and said they were so fortunate. Nerissa couldn't stop talking about their accommodations and how magnificent the safari was. Shawn had told Rob about the family they met in Rio and about their living conditions, not to mention the danger they had lived in. Shawn said the kids and Pa were doing an awesome job helping the family rebuild to the highest standard as possible. The two men that came from church in Niagara were getting things done at a phenomenal rate. They were going back to see how things looked. Dad couldn't believe it would take twelve hours to get to Rio from here.

"We will be out of your hair Rob, by morning at 8 am," Shawn reported.

Rob was a nice guy and would never say it, but Shawn figured he spent a lot of time with people, making them comfortable on their trips to Africa. Just like he had done for them this trip, going the extra mile and even booking the safari for them. It would not go unnoticed. They were sorry to have missed his wife, but knew they would catch up with her in Niagara, on one of her trips back.

The airport was already busy as they arrived. Soon Nerissa would see Josh and Pa!

CHAPTER 22

Dynamite in the Tunnels

The information leaked to the power plant, worked. There was a very small piece in the newspaper stating that the power plant was clearing out some of the old dynamite that was used in the building of the plant and tunnels. Nothing more was said about it being German dynamite. They announced some roads would be closed for a time and the foot traffic would also be halted. Bee reported to us while we were waiting at the airport. The paper said they had armed guards protecting the work crew as they had spotted a cougar. She said the cougar part was played up, probably to scare people. Another person had said they took a shot at a cougar and they thought they hit it. They warned people to be aware of the dangerous animal. Bee was concerned about that. She thought she should go down into the tunnels to see if Girl was hit.

Mom sternly forbid it. "What if it was that wild male cougar? You should not do that. What if the men get into the tunnels and find you? What if something happens?"

Nerissa continued on with her warnings. Bee said she would not do anything stupid and that Kelly was by her side. She told them not to worry. She would report back and tell them what the paper said next.

Bee had to see what Girl was up to. She knew where the stun gun, flares and so on where in the tunnel. She told Grammy and Grammpy that she was going to stay at Carly's for a few days. Carly needed cheering up as she was missing Dustin. This was true, but Bee was not going to see her. Kelly said that he was going home to retrieve some school material left behind and was getting a ride with the Amish driver. If the senior couple needed anything, Vanessa or Barry would be glad to help them out. Bee's car would be left, too, as Carly was supposed to pick her up. Bee asked Barry and Vanessa if they could check in on her grandparents until she returned. They were happy to.

Kelly was ecstatic to be on his first real mission in the tunnel. Bee had experienced many. They locked the doors, although the elderly couple could easily access the house and of course, that was just fine. They took all their supplies of food and so on. She thought of Josh's exploration bag, which she thought was so useless. She realized it would contain all those little items she might need. She packed her own bag with antiseptic cream, tweezers, medication, needle and thread and many other items.

They went down through Pa's study. The underground living area held sleeping bags and more. Their backpacks were full. They had two high-powered flashlights and three smaller ones attached to their packs.

"I don't know where we will find Girl and the family," admitted Bee.

Kelly replied, "I hope she isn't hurt. I don't know if the younger two will survive without her!"

They walked to the bottom where the cougar's den was. Bee called, but no cougar appeared.

"Girl," she called again.

They walked a little further and checked the first outside ridge. They had an eerie feeling like they were being watched.

"Do you feel someone watching us?" asked Bee.

"Yes, it feels so creepy."

They went back into the tunnel and Bee stopped to shine the light all the way around, as did Kelly.

"Over there," whispered Bee.

"What did you see?" Kelly asked as he moved his light to join her directed light.

Bee saw fur, so she ran over, not thinking of the wild cougar. Kelly was right behind her. She was just thinking about Girl, Sweetheart and Halfpint.

"Oh look, it is Sweetheart!" Bee cried out.

Sweetheart came out from hiding and started to lick Bee's face. There were no wounds on her. Bee wondered where the other two were. Girl would never leave the younger ones.

"Where's Girl?" asked Bee, as if Sweetheart could understand.

Sweetheart walked away and stopped to look back. Bee recognized that the kitten wanted her to follow.

"Come Kelly, we need to follow her," Bee exclaimed.

They followed for quite some time as they had to reach the tomb cavern and entered in the direction of the tunnel to the dynamite and electric plant. They knew they could not go to the end as the men were working removing the dynamite. Sweetheart seemed to be taking her time and they kept on following. Bee expressed that she hoped Girl was at the large ridge where there was water. It looked like they were going that way. It seemed like hours as they passed the carcass, now only a clean skeleton. At least it didn't stink anymore. Sweetheart sniffed the carcass as if she was familiar with the scent. When Sweetheart turned the corner going to the edge of the gorge, Bee knew where she was going and ran until she came to the water bridge.

"Don't worry," she said as she stopped.

The water level had gone down so they could walk on the rock ledge without getting wet. Kelly followed, being warned not to bump his head. Now she moved quickly. There was no one in the open topped cave! As she exited the rock enclosure, she almost screamed. It was Girl with Halfpint by her side. They were both bloody. Bee opened her supplies and Kelly asked what she needed. "Get me some water!" she demanded. She had a collapsible pail that came in very handy. Kelly ran for water. Halfpint came to Bee and seemed fine, although a total bloody mess. Bee wondered where she was hurt.

"Kelly, can you wash Halfpint down and check her over?" Bee asked.

Girl did not move! Bee carefully examined her. Sweetheart came and licked her mother's face. Bee found the wound. It looked like a bullet wound. Bee didn't know much about this, but knew she should remove the bullet and stop the bleeding.

"If Halfpint is alright, help me with Girl. She is badly hurt and I need help moving her over," Bee exclaimed.

"Halfpint looks fine," reported Kelly. "After a couple of dunks in the pail she was clean!"

Girl was dead weight and they could hardly manage to pull her away from the side of the rock wall. Bee needed access to the wound so Kelly helped her. She cleaned the wound thoroughly and Kelly ran for more water. Bee took out her medical supplies and started to look for her tweezers. She knew she brought them. Bee looked frazzled so Kelly took the bag out of her shaking hands.

"Here you are," said Kelly handing her the tweezers. "Just take a minute and breathe, you have time, we will do our best, okay?" he reassured her.

Bee pulled herself together and started to look for the bullet. Kelly shone the light into the wound for a better view.

"There it is, I see it," she exclaimed.

As she dug and probed for the bullet, she finally grasped it. Bee pulled it up and it was out. The wound was still profusely bleeding. She put pressure on the wound, as that is what you see on medical shows.

"Kelly, can you put pressure on this for me? I need to get the needle and thread ready, as well as the antibiotic cream."

 Of course, he obliged. She got her equipment ready and started to prepare herself for the job. She hoped the bleeding would stop internally. Bee did not know how to sew up the wound on the inside. If they had internet, she could look it up. She tried to get some water into Girl's mouth but she was not swallowing. Kelly was putting pressure on the wound with a bandage to soak up the blood while Bee was getting her courage up.

Kelly decided to take charge of the situation.

"I can do this," he said.

He had watched and assisted his dad handle many emergencies on the farm as he grew up. He took some of the emergency gun powder from his back pack and put just a thin layer into the wound. He then lit it with his lighter. Having a damp cloth ready, he put it over the flame to put it out.

"Now we need to close it up and watch for infection."

Bee was ready with the thread and needle and was glad to do the rest. Her stitches would hold the wound together until it healed.

Halfpint tried to drink out of the pail of bloody water. Bee quickly took the pail and dumped it, but realized the little one was hungry and probably hadn't eaten since Girl got hurt. She took out a bottle of her water and poured some into Halfpint's mouth. She drank like a trooper and Bee wondered if she would lap water. She poured some in her hand and Halfpint didn't know how to lap it. She poured more into the kitten's mouth, and she guzzled it down until she was satisfied. She would have to learn to lap water. Bee put out a shallow dish of water for her. Sweetheart came and had some. Halfpint watched. Before this she did not need to care for herself as Girl had nursed her and cared for her every need. Kelly checked the wound and the bleeding had stopped. The antibacterial cream was applied and now they would watch and see what would happen. Girl was still not moving and they were concerned. She would need time to regain her strength. Animals mended quickly and Bee was sure Girl would too. The cubs played in the tall grasses beside their mother, who looked like she was sleeping. Her fur was covered in red with a large bandage on it. Now that she was relaxing a little more, Bee noticed it was quite a unique picture. She took one with her phone. Later on, she took one of Kelly, Halfpint jumping on his back, while he was checking Girl's wound. Bee laughed at the sight as he grabbed the kitten. She made up their beds in the open topped cave and was thankful for a warm summer evening.

"How is she doing, Kelly?" she asked.

"Still no bleeding."

"We will know when she wakes up and soon, I hope," Bee mumbled.

"I have some food, if you would like to eat before it gets dark," Bee suggested.

"Of course, I am hungry after all of our work," he said, laughing.

She had made a small picnic and even had a small red and white checkered table cloth along with two matching napkins, sandwiches, pickles, Grammy's cookies and a thermos of coffee.

"Wow, how did you get that together?" he asked. "Will we have enough for tomorrow?"

"I made sure we would not run out of food for at least three days, just in case," Bee replied.

"Great, then let's eat," he said.

He remembered to pray for Girl and her family and Bee and her family and the group that went to South America, as well as blessing the food. Bee loved how he was a take-charge kind of guy and did whatever, to make life work. She told him of the first time Dad and the others were here in this unique cavern. Bee had always hoped that Kelly would be able to see it too.

"The first time I was here, was the most perfect evening and the first time the group met Halfpint. We thought she was dead. The moon shone brightly that night, with all the mystery and romance it could provide. The only problem was, I had no one to be romantic with. I do now!" Bee said, as she laughed.

Their sandwich was delicious and Sweetheart came to see what caught her scent.

"I think she is hungry," added Kelly.

"Here you go girl," he said, offering his half-eaten sandwich to Sweetheart.

Sweetheart grabbed it and seemed to enjoy it. Bee gave Kelly half of her sandwich. She was living on love these days. They checked the trio once more and gave Halfpint some more water. Girl was doing well too.

"I think that is all we can do for the night except check them once in a while," Bee suggested.

They wrapped themselves, each in their own sleeping bag. Neither one of them would do anything to betray the trust Bee's parents had put in them. Looking at the stars above, they talked about their future. The two had wants, dreams and hopes and took the time to articulate how they felt regarding them all. They talked until Bee dozed off and Kelly went to check on the cougar family once more. All was well, so he went to sleep. He was a little concerned about Girl and the severity of her wound.

Bee jumped up as the sun rose, to check on Girl. Kelly was already by the animal's side. He was encouraged that she wasn't bleeding anymore, but there was still no movement. They were concerned and Bee decided to crush and mix some travel antibiotics. They were left from the mission trip Dad took to Africa and did not need. He was going to take them back to the pharmacy to get rid of, but forgot. Bee saw them and grabbed them with her medical supplies. She read the container. She decided to see if Girl would swallow some water first. Maybe today she would be just that much better. Kelly held her head up so it would trickle down her throat.

"Yes, she is swallowing!" Bee exclaimed.

She quickly mixed the medicine with water and poured it down Girl's throat. She swallowed it. They would give her another dose at noon and one at nighttime. It was just one little step towards health. Halfpint was playful and kept looking for something to satisfy her hunger. We gave her some more water. Kelly loved his milk but was ready to sacrifice it. From a water bottle he poured it down Halfpint's throat. She seemed to inhale the easy meal of milk.

"We need to get her to drink on her own," Bee mused.

"It would keep her alive if something happened to Girl," Kelly agreed.

Sweetheart, of course, went to the pool to drink and enjoyed her human food for breakfast. They wondered if she had learned to hunt, until we saw her lying on the far side near the rock wall tearing something apart. They went to look and there she was enjoying her second breakfast. The first one just didn't satisfy her. She must have gone hunting last night or early this morning and caught a rodent. They were so pleased as she tore at the carcass. She would make it no matter what. At noon, they gave Girl another dose of antibiotic. Bee would guarantee her Dad would never have thought of this scenario!

They put some milk in the shallow container so Halfpint could work at her drinking skills. She kept on sniffing the milk and walking around the dish. Sweetheart came over and started to lap. Suddenly the kitten started to lap the milk too. They were so ecstatic! It was the first step in Halfpint's independence. They knew it would take a lot more, but were grateful for the baby steps. It was around sunset and they were giving Girl her medication when she opened her eyes.

"Hi Girl," Bee soothed with her voice. "How are you doing?"

She was petting Girl and it seemed like she was responding.

Sweetheart and Halfpint came over to show their support. It was good for Girl as she licked them, although not for long. They made the younger family members leave the parent alone so she could get stronger. This night would make a huge improvement on Girl, or so we hoped.

In the morning, Bee was the first to be up and ran out to check on the cougars. There in front of Girl lay a fresh muskrat. It was ugly to me, but would taste good to the cougar. There was another one that Sweetheart was working on. Sweetheart must be a good hunter, thought Bee. She has learned well.

The medication was wearing off of Girl and she was waking up. She sat up and started to eat her breakfast. Bee couldn't watch as she devoured her prepared prey. It was too gory a sight for her. By this time, Kelly stood by her side in amazement. He suggested they leave the family to enjoy this moment together, in whichever manner they chose.

"I think you are right," she agreed as she took Kelly's hand.

Kelly and Bee sat and took some time before they ate their breakfast in their rock enclosure. The previous scene was too fresh in their minds They were absolutely convinced that Girl would be just fine. Kelly said he would put the antibiotics in her water later. They would try to get another day's worth into her.

The plan was to get back tonight. It wouldn't matter if it were day or night, as the tunnels were dark all the time. By mid-afternoon the adult cougar seemed so much better. She even took a walk inside the tunnel to the water pool and had a long drink. When she returned, we gave the last dose of antibiotic. She took it well in a piece of bread. As if it was all too much, she lay down again. Halfpint took advantage and returned to her adoptive mom to feed. They felt we had done our job well and the cougars would make it. Hopefully no infection would set into Girl's wounds and she would totally recover.

"I hate to leave them!" Bee whined.

"Look around. Is there enough room here to do all the things you want to in life?" he asked.

As she looked around, she said, "Of course not!"

"Well then, I suggest we keep this as a place where special memories are made, ones that will be in our minds for the rest of our lives," he added.

"Awe, that is so sweet, Kelly. Thank you for being you. I know we have to leave, but I needed a push," she conceded.

They made sure everything was packed up and gave the cougars their last pats good-bye.

"Now Sweetheart, we are counting on you!" she commanded, sounding like her mom when she left.

For some reason, the backpacks seemed heavier than when they arrived. They were careful to take all the remnants of dirty gauze and so on wrapped in a small garbage bag. There should never be a trace of a human visit to the area. It would compromise their secret. It would take a few hours to get back and they moved with a steady pace through the tunnels. They were almost at the cavern of bones and heard screeching. It sounded scary and haunting as it echoed through the tunnels.

"What is that?" Bee whispered.

Kelly looked around the corner. There were swarms of bats flying around everywhere. Of course, it was night and they fed during these hours. They were coming and going through the tunnels above. That was where we had to go!

"What are we going to do?" Bee asked.

"Let me think," Kelly said.

"Bats are great for cleaning the air of bugs, and they do not harm people; especially the bats in Ontario," Kelly relayed. "How do you feel about going through this cavern and up the stairs to the upper tunnels?"

Bee replied, "Through the flying bats?"

She was terrified and had heard horror stories of bats getting tangled in peoples' hair and biting them, giving humans rabies. Kelly had a plan to protect Bee. He would put on his climbing gloves, cover as much of his face and body as he could, and so would Bee. With her hood up, she did not have to worry about her hair being tangled up with bats.

"I will hold the stun gun ahead of us in the air and use it as often as I need. The bats fly by sonar and that might interfere with their transmitting our waves. Did you know that they transmit from their mouth to the object and then receive with their ears?"

"No, I didn't and that is cool but gross," Bee replied.

"I am willing to give it a try," she said.

They covered every part of their body that they could. Bee wrapped Kelly's entire arm down to his leather gloves with the checkered tablecloth. She used a roll of medical tap to fasten the material.

Bee held the light to guide their steps. They did not have to worry until they got nearer to the top. Suddenly the bats were all around them, darting at them.

Bee screamed, and her flashlight shone all over the place! Kelly started to use the stun gun and it seemed to work.

"Bee, are you okay and ready to move forward?" he asked.

"Yes," she whimpered.

"Put the light where I can see!" he ordered.

"Okay."

They kept walking at a good pace and Kelly continued to activate the stun gun. He always pointed to the rock wall away from the bats as not to hurt them. The bats would go for it instead of the two intruders. Saying that, they were diving at his hand continually. It didn't even bother him as the gun was nicely doing the trick. He should have been protected enough to withstand bat bites. They reached the top and into the next tunnel. Bee was so relieved. She was shaking and felt this was the scariest thing she had ever endured. She was so glad to get back to the safety of the inner tunnel.

"Is it normal to have that many bats in one area?" she asked.

"Actually, only when they swarm once a year at this time. They all get together male and female and show the young where the hibernation site is. The females have a chance to mate and the males try to have as many offspring as possible. That number of bats would have been bats from other hibernation sites, as well as this one."

This area would usually have bats, but not this many Kelly added.

"Do you mean there are bats here all the time?" Bee exclaimed!

Kelly answered, "Yes, but you have never seen them before, right?"

With a nod she conceded that was true and she would try not worry about it.

Back at home in the old mansion, they regrouped, unpacked the equipment and showered. The first thing Bee wanted to do was call

Mom. She would be worried sick about them. They tried to be very quiet as they were not supposed to be home until the next morning.

Calling from the upstairs phone, Bee told her mother and father all that had happened. They were proud of the job the two did and thanked Kelly for staying by Bee's side the whole way. Of course, that was a given, he replied to them.

"How is your project going?" Bee asked with interest.

Dad was so excited and gave her all the details. "Sewer, plumbing, electrical, the walls, doors and windows are all in. I cannot believe how quickly these men are working. When we got here, there were so many men from the community helping, you could hardly move. I don't know how Pa kept them all going. Your mother is already helping Lauren pick her tiles, appliances, beds and so on. Lauren would like to start the guesthouse as soon as possible and thinks this is a good chance to accessorize with a Canadian flair to attract the right tourists. You would love this part, Bee. You are good at it too. Decorating is your forte'! They are going to paint the inside while the wrap-around decks are being completed. You should see the rooftop! It is already finished and furnished so the workers have a place to eat and crash for a break. It is so nice. You would love it, Bee. Oh, I have to tell you, your Mom got a hold of a picture of the Kempt family's mother and father and had it enlarged and framed for the wall. She will give it to them before we leave. We were shocked at how much like her mother Lauren looked, and Joel looks like his father. Manny is a good mix of both parents. You will have to come and meet them someday."

"I hope I can. It would be nice to meet Lauren. She sounds so nice. I think we would get along well," Bee said.

"You would love these guys, Bee. They are so much like my own children, but have had a very tough life. They have made the best of it, always picking themselves up and going on, no matter what."

Bee reported that they would check in with Grammy and Grammpy in the morning. She thought it would be good if someone told them the secret, as it was becoming more difficult to keep from them. Dad said he would consider it when he got back.

"How are Josh, Mac and Mark doing?" Bee asked.

"Oh, they are having the time of their lives. They are so tanned and working at least eight hours a day. They have become very good friends with everyone here and I assume will miss this place when they have to leave."

"So sorry about the wasted trip to Africa," Bee sympathized.

"On the contrary, Bee, it was a very short but reenergizing trip for your Mother and I. We had a wonderful time just concentrating on us for a change," he replied enthusiastically.

"That is so nice to hear Dad. You and Mom don't get much time together without having to think of others. Look at your Europe trip!" She reported. "Well, I will say goodnight, Dad. Give my love to all," Bee announced as she sent them an audible kiss, and hung up.

CHAPTER 23

More Secrets Revealed

Dad and Mom were looking through some more of the family albums when they came across a picture of two soldiers in uniform. It was valuable how people wrote on the back of photos for generations after them to be able to recognize who was on the photo. This one had a picture of Herman, the family father and a man named Helmut. It said, "To be stationed together on a secret mission."

This was a breakthrough. We had a picture of the soldier that the prisoners and our relative put all their hope in. We made a copy of both sides of the photo. Josh felt so bad that he had treated the skeleton so poorly and had to carry it in a sack to retrieve it. We had a photo of the mystery soldier! We were sure the soldier had no family. The prisoners would have left some money to the soldier's family if so. When there was an absence of family they continually gave their portion to the rest of the fellow prisoners.

Mac was sleeping at the house with Lauren. They were now good friends even though they were separated by a few years. They found age was not a deterrent, and maturity and interests formed their bond. Mac enjoyed waking up to the magnificent view every morning! Lauren and Mac had their morning coffee on the rooftop, even before the workers started to hammer and work. We were afraid we were not going to get Mac home with us. Joel was also becoming a very good friend and they would often be seen in deep conversations in the evenings.

"Look at how this house looks!" Nerissa announced, as the last work was done on the decks. Shawn had financed the whole job knowing full well it would kick start their family life. He was beside himself at the sight of the building. It looked like a mansion compared to all the houses around it. There was news of wealthy people buying up these dilapidated homes to put up new ones. At least the Wolfgang family was in on the ground floor of the rising cost of this neighborhood. Lauren would have her rooms full in no time and be making money. They now owned two good buildings in good neighborhoods. Their work was almost done in this home.

Nerissa, Mac and Lauren shopped for beds and bedding. Lauren was an awesome seamstress and got some curtains from hotels that were being remodeled. She made bedspreads and black-out window covers to match. Mac painted some night stands they retrieved from the hotel dumpster, along with some worn upholstery chairs. The frames were painted in complimentary colors and Lauren put new material on them, also salvaged from recycled curtains. Everyone thought they were new. They also got unique pieces of wood from the beach and bleached them. They made unique hangings for the walls. Photos of the homes views were framed. After drilling a hole into the driftwood and screwing it to a stand, they used the old lamp hardware from the dumpster and painted the shades. It cost next to nothing. Joel and the guys went to buy three small fridges for the guest-rooms. Each room had hooks for their own colored towels, complimenting the décor of the rooms. There were old chairs and a small table, all refurbished with a fresh coat of white Milk Paint and newly covered cushions. The table had stones from the beach placed in waves like that of the walkway at the beach. The exterior of the house was a white plaster, so Lauren wanted to give it a crisp white, black, and grey with a pop of color. The front door was painted a bright red. She covered the outside cushions in a large red floral print. It looked stunning. Manny and Josh and Mark found an old stone planter and literally dragged it up to the house as it was so heavy. The planter looked stunning painted black. It stood in front of the white house beside the red door. Lauren was beside herself when the house was all pulled together. The God-sent men from Niagara went back with an invitation to come and stay anytime. They thanked the young family for making their stay so enjoyable. The men from the community took pride in the home they helped reconstruct. They hoped one day they would have a chance at changing their lives too. Their life in the past was so poor and it made their present life seem so very extravagant; more than they could have imagined.

Dad knew that, but they deserved better and were ready to move forward. The timing was right to make them financially independent. Maybe Lauren could go to designer school and fulfill her dream one day and Joel should take those psychology courses he was interested in. Adam would have time to play instead of working after school. Manny could finish his schooling and decide what he wanted to do with his life, besides studying about Canada.

They were told that the gift of the picture with their ancestor, the German soldier, proved he was in actuality a hero. He assisted men imprisoned for years, before the Germans killed them all. They knew Dad was a researcher, so they accepted it and left the news at that, asking no more questions. They felt good about their roots and the blood that flowed through their veins. Adam was the only one not sure he was a good person. He did not realize that his family had already lived as good people before they knew where they came from. Pa told him it doesn't matters who "you" are! It is how you live your life that really matters.

The advertisement was set up online for them and with their new computer they would be able to stay in touch with us as well as book their guests. It was definitely another bitter sweet good-bye.

Dad had another plan to reveal to his family once they got home. He wondered if they would be ready to travel so soon after they returned home.

Home felt good, even though the family had a lovely time away. They caught up with Bee and Kelly in regards to their journey and of course with Grammy and Grammpy. Dad had decided to tell the elderly couple about the secret of the mansion. It was a long story and took quite some time. Dad wanted to take them down to the tunnels, showing them the access, and Grammpy confided that he had already been down there. He got stopped at a door that needed a key! Dad was shocked and it confirmed once again that this man was as sharp as a tack and nothing got by him. He would take them into the tunnels another time.

"How did you find it? "Dad asked.

"I put two and two together and it did not add up. People said they were coming and going but I did not see them. People appeared in the house and the biggest thing was, when I found a secret door in our place that took us down to a nice tunnel. It all makes sense now: why the body was exhumed, and people disappeared, and why Bee and Nissa came to visit. We noticed the bruises on Bee, but didn't say anything."

"Well now you know," Dad said.

Mom added, "The danger should be over, unless the wrong people find out and think there is more gold. You know how people get about money! The gold had been cashed into currency and there were a few very healthy bank accounts out there. We were waiting for a coin collector to send word. He was very interested in purchasing the coins and then it would all be done."

The family gathered around after they had finished their private conversation. Mark and Mac were called to see if they could join them for dessert. Mac's mom and dad asked if she wanted to move in since she spent so much time with our family.

We laughed when she told us, until Mom said," I would feel the same if you Josh and Bee would be away to Mac's house all the time."

We never looked at it that way, but it made sense. Josh remembered how he felt when his dad was gone all the time. It left a void.

Dad started off with, "Because of our previous conversation, I don't think this will go over too well. But it is something I would like you to experience."

"What Dad? Just come out with it!" encouraged Josh.

"Well, Dustin will be here with his family, sooner than we thought. The home they live in now may change a lot. I would like you all to see who some of these men from the tunnels were. I want you to experience the Schwartz home before everything changes. They were special men before they worked as prisoners in our tunnels. I would like us to go to Germany and to Venice. There will be three stops in Germany and one in Venice. Of course we can be tourists while we are over there."

CHAPTER 24

Mac's Affirmation

"Do you mean me too?" asked Mac, as she did not have ancestors that died in the tunnel.

"Of course. Especially you. Weren't you and Josh the first ones to find the tunnels and rooms down there?" Dad reaffirmed. "You and Josh got the ball rolling in order to find Pa. We will never forget the part you played in all of this."

Mac was overwhelmed with the praise given to her and spoke with teary eyes, "Thanks, I just did what any one of you would have done."

"And that is exactly Dad's point, Mac. You did as we would have and that is why you are one of us," Josh confirmed.

Dad wanted it to give closure to the descendants of the prisoners. The final closure would happen later and he would not announce that yet. Of course everyone would be trying to get that out of him, but they all realized they would find out when the time was right. We thought we should leave next week.

"You are all welcome to come as we would love you to join us," Dad said. "I will wait to book when I hear back from you." Everyone was buzzing.

"Now Dad, I hope you are leaving some time for Kelly and myself to get married! It will be soon, remember?" Bee said.

"I would never forget that, Bee. It is the most special occasion that we are participating in this year and I am sure it will be beautiful," Dad announced.

Grammpy had started plans to get the gazebo into its former glory. The gazebo looked much like the one restored in Niagara-on-the-Lake at the water's edge. He ordered exact replicas of the old wood from his Amish friend back in Lancaster. Next week it would get a face lift.

"Grammpy, we would like both of you to come along with us." Pa remarked.

"Oh I thank you, but Grammy and I don't like to travel and will hold the home-front together."

After everyone's pleading and the couple not budging, they gave in to them staying home. Mom and Bee had made all the wedding arrangement in no time and Bee had specific ideas on what she expected. She wanted a simple, yet memorable wedding. Everything would have purpose and meaning for Kelly and herself. It would be different than others as form didn't mean much to them.

She had already sent the invitations. Grammy would keep track of the responses arriving in the mail and Carly those that arrived by email.

"By the way, Mark, your mother can go too!" suggested Mom.

"Thanks!" Mark replied, over the top with joy.

"You can have your parents call me regarding the plans. I would be glad to meet with them too," Dad added.

Everyone was buzzing. They were all going to Europe. Kelly was going too and it would be so exciting. Bee thought it was too bad the wedding wasn't before the trip; they could make it their honeymoon. As soon as she thought it, she dismissed the thought, as who wanted to honeymoon with the whole family around? Bee loved her family, but sure didn't want them around on this special time of memory making.

Soon after the meeting on Europe, Dad received a call from Barry.

"You didn't tell me you won the lottery!" Barry said.

"I didn't in that way Barry, but when Pa came back to us and we had to deal with wondering if Omz was alive or not, I decided that we would not waste our lives not enjoying ourselves with the ones we loved. Mac and Mark seem to be one of those, Barry and I hope you don't mind sharing Mac with us."

"We are happy she has found good trustworthy friends. I will tell you what; we would like to make memories with our daughter too.

Could we go too with the understanding that we also pay for Mac," Barry insisted.

"That is not necessary," Shawn replied to his friend.

They discussed the trip and the plans Dad had for the group. Barry was going to coincide his family trip with Shawn's and then branch off to do other things. That sounded wonderful and they would plan parts of the trip together. There were only a few places he needed Mac to see and she could spend the rest of the time with her parents.

Mark came in the door with his mother close behind. She knocked before she came in.

"Is its true you want to go to Europe?" she inquired.

Dad filled her in and said she could pay him back whenever, to put her mind at ease. She just could not get her head around the cost that Dad was willing to put out. It was going to be an awesome time. He told her if she had places she wanted to see, he would advance her some more money and she could visit them too. Shawn would give her the itinerary and she could add to it. He wondered if she knew the town where her ancestors were from. She would have a chance to see it firsthand. It was settled. Their travel agent would be pleased with this booking. There were eleven people in the group. They would fly into Hamburg Germany and home from Venice. The fourteen days' trip would cover what they needed to do.

Grammpy had lumber delivered and now knew the purpose of the gazebo and why the stairs had to stay. He would have work done by the time the travelers were back. He was aware to keep the secret entrance hidden, but accessible.

CHAPTER 25

Not Who He Thought He Was

Getting to Germany was awesome. Mac and Mark's family, making a group of five, hooked up on shuttles and road transportation. Dad booked a large van as we were six people. It gave us just enough room. We were warned to travel very light and we did. Everyone had just a carry-on or a backpack.

Our rented Airbnb house would be our home base for four days. It was modest but clean and comfortable. We had all the bedrooms we needed and pull-out couches. With a full kitchen and four bathrooms, it was a deal.

We said we would go to the homestead first, as Pa was anxious to see it again. Everyone was welcome to join us if they wanted to. Mark and Mac were on board, of course, as they knew this was where Josh and Bee's descendants came from. Mark and Mac's parents decided to drive out with us and have a look at this place too. It would give them a picture of the German countryside. They would look around town today and leave first thing in the morning. The ladies decided to bring a picnic lunch for the group.

There were many small villages along the way and the sunshine accented the white homes and clean sparkling windows, dressed in lace toppers and pristine gardens. They stopped at a little town and visited a bakery. Everything smelled and looked delicious. Besides sweets, they purchased a couple of loaves of fresh bread. There was an old meat shop, which they also decided to visit. The first thing that caught their eyes were the pig ears, tails, and feet. The kids couldn't imagine what that would taste like. There was a cow's tongue and fish still wearing their heads and eyes in their sockets! It was gross. We bought some liver pâté, salami, black forest ham, and smoked eel, as Pa said he remembered eating it when he was a boy. After all, it was all about remembering the past and enjoying the present. Looking at the various cheeses, it was difficult to decide which varieties to buy. Josh spotted the pickles sitting in a barrel. He, of course, wanted some of those too. The sales clerk let us try them before we purchased a small pail full. The potato salad was our last selection. This would be a delicious German lunch. Out of nowhere, Nerissa pulled out these cooler bags, that you just had to crack, and they got cold. She thought of everything. When they arrived at the old homestead, they found they could drive their cars right to the house. Jervaih had cleared all the trees and brush to make a nice clearing all the way up to the home. Mom and Dad were so surprised that the roof had already been repaired and Lovlyn had planted a garden. They had a rustic shed beside the house that resembled a cast-away that someone might have given to them. A very pregnant looking Lovlyn greeted the group with open arms. Clara shyly followed behind her mother. When Clara saw Nerissa, she remembered her and darted right for her, wanting a lift into her arms. Nerissa was delighted that she remembered her and of course, obliged. Jervaih and Lovlyn knew that the group would arrive. Everyone was greeted warmly with hugs and kisses to both sides of the face. The chatter was wild until they all personally met. They convinced Dad, Pa, Josh and Bee to go into the house first. Dad was taken by surprise. It was just like before, as Lovlyn had left it as it was, only fixing the ceiling.

Pa looked at the dishes in the old cabinet.

He said, "This is the cup I drank from as a young boy. It was an aluminum cup made of prevalent material of that time. Pa walked into the bedroom where he slept as a boy. The memories just kept flooding in. It was so many years ago and yet in this house it seemed like yesterday. Pa went to the simple looking fireplace. He knew he remembered something about standing right in this spot. He thought back.

"So, you know I caught my father lifting the floorboards right here. He didn't know I was watching him and when he looked up it was too late. I was looking right at him. He went to get a hammer and said he was fixing these boards," Pa spoke, contemplating.

"See, the nails are still in here," he said as he kneeled to touch them.

"Well, do you think there is something down there that we should see?" asked Bee, now curious.

Jervaih went to get a hammer. He knew interesting things happened around this family. Last time they found the letter from Pa's parents. What were they going to find this time?

Pa took the pry end of the hammer and started to pull out the two nails, one on each end. He carefully lifted the board, with great anticipation, not knowing what lay beneath the floor. Dad was right there beside Pa, not being able to stand the suspense. It was a small old album. Pa lifted it out carefully. Under it lay an old Bible. He opened the Bible wondering why this antique was left behind.

The door opened and many voices sounded as they interrupted the moment. The others were coming in with Mom and talking loudly. Dad quickly got up and stated that they needed a few more minutes. They saw Pa on the floor with the old relic in his hands. Barry had everyone back up and return outside. Vanessa said she would prepare the picnic at the old table outside and they should join them when they were ready. Mac and Mark wondered what they were missing and should they be inside too? Mom gave Clara back to Lovlyn and stayed inside wondering why Pa was on the floor. Dad filled her in and I went to sit with Pa on the floor. The Bible had a letter in it. It was from Pa's mother and father. It stated that they wanted to leave a part of their past behind. It was the part where Pa was born and they took him in. Everyone had surprised looks on their faces.

The story went like this: a young girl came begging for food. She was running from someone who wanted to kill her and she was hiding. Of course, Antonie Wittfoot gave her a good meal and a place to stay. She had two books and she carried them wrapped in an old cloth. Her mother, also in hiding somewhere else, as she feared for her life, told her to keep these two books safe as well as hidden. The young girl said she came from a family of great wealth but had not experienced it in her lifetime. She was given to an elderly, cruel man as a wife to hide her. She was abused and starved by this man. Her mother had stressed to her to hide these pictures as they would prove who she was.

The cruel man beat and forced himself on her many times and kept her hidden away even though she found herself expecting a child. She thought in one of the last beatings he would kill her unborn child next time, so she ran away with all that she could carry. Where she came from, life was that way. You did what you were told and a woman had no right to express herself. The young woman was beaten in spirit as well as physically. She begged Antonie to stay until she had her child and then she would leave. Of course, the couple agreed and would even help her afterwards. Wilhelmina, the young girl stayed for another three months until the baby was born. It was a beautiful baby boy. This baby she named Harry, before he was even born.

The letter continued to say, "Yes you were not born to us but rather given to us by God."

Wilhelmina died at childbirth having had too many complications. Antonie and Herbert were left with no choice but to raise this child as their own. The letter expressed how fortunate they felt to have this opportunity, as they could not have children of their own. It was an adorable child and the whole family enjoyed nurturing him. The house was filled daily with joy, gratitude and laughter. Reading on, Pa said they left these pieces of history here, as they had no legal adoption papers. They were immigrating to Canada. They would adopt their child legally in Canada. They hoped the papers would be found by the appropriate people one day. It was never done in malice but out of love and need.

Pa rubbed his chin and said, "Well I'll be. I'm adopted. Now I know what it feels like to have that bomb dropped on you."

Josh asked, "Are you okay, Pa? Can I get you something?"

"You can help me up, Josh, before my knees seize up," Pa replied.

"Sure thing," Josh answered, as he and Bee both took the hands of the distraught senior and helped him rise to his feet.

He sat on an old chair and started to look at the pictures of his biological family. They looked Russian. He didn't even know his last name at birth. He looked on the back of some of the photos. Nothing. He wished he could at least find a picture of his biological mother. Pa went back to the Bible. At the back was a photo of a young teen girl. This had to be his mother. Why would it be there? On the back was a name: Wilhelmina Anastasia Romanov.

"Was she from the house of Romanov, of Russia, from St. Petersburg?" Pa was puzzled.

It was a good thing they left these papers behind.

"Are you rich, Pa?" asked Josh.

"You can bet I am, son! Not because of this. I have learned through the years how rich I am and more than that. What makes a man rich, is not money, it is a family like God has given me years ago. Do you know what I am saying, Josh?"

"Of course, Pa, it is how I feel to and I am only a kid,"

It was time to leave Pa and let him digest his thoughts. We went outside and joined the others. It looked like a party and the food looked so good. Everyone was kind and let us compose ourselves for a moment. All we told them was that Pa had just found out that he was adopted. Everyone was shocked and agreed it was God's best plan. Pa gave so much to everyone there.

In a while, Pa came out and felt free to talk about his experience in the house. People went in and out looking at the homestead and Pa's newly discovered books. Pa kept the picture of his mother with the signature on the back and didn't let anyone see it.

They had a look under the sink, where Pa's mother hid a letter for her brothers-in-law, if they should return. The floorboards, where Pa had found proof of his adoption, was also open. Barry was intrigued with the secrets they had uncovered. Mac wondered what he would say if he knew all the other secrets. They took their time and enjoyed the country home. Jervaih ensured them that if anything else was found, he would make sure that they got it. Shawn, of course, knew he would.

Lovlyn announced, "We received a wedding invitation. We would love to come but I cannot travel because of the baby coming!"

It was understandable and we accepted that. Mom said she would send lots of pictures, as it would be a lovely time of celebration. They thanked the couple and left the food with them. Jervaih told Pa to come back anytime. Pa had another opportunity to see the homestead and to take a few of his family possessions with him.

Dad noticed the Bible he had left behind last visit, laying there on the table. He asked Jervaih how the reading was going. He replied he was almost done.

"It is like a wonder drug! It lifts you high and shows you things you were not aware of," he proclaimed with enthusiasm.

Dad was happy with the progress and left the rest to God and his word. He just added the Bible was good for the whole family.

We left with hugs and waves and felt loved by our new friends. They had shared our past and present in the short time we've known them.

CHAPTER 26

The Death Walk

Dad announced to everyone that we were going to a town near Bremen tomorrow. The destination would be most interesting if they wanted to accompany us It would be something that no one should miss. Mac and Mark were already slotted to go. Angela, Barry and Vanessa had no hesitation after today as the new found treasures and information sparked their intrigue. Barry knew Shawn and Pa did investigative work, but didn't realize how far back they dug. He asked what the circumstances were on this case. Shawn implied he was hired to find a descendent who might have some artifacts.

They would leave early the next day. Nerissa and Shawn were so excited for their family to meet Mary and her two boys, Mitchell, as well as see Dustin again.

They arrived at the house and of course said hello to "Mrs. Semph." She just stared at all the people visiting Mary Schwartz. It was like she counted them as they got out of the vehicles. Mary welcomed us in with her fresh apple strudel and cinnamon buns. She had them nicely displayed on the counter on her best platters. A very good cup of coffee accompanied the sweets. The boys were excited for all of the group to see their treasure. Dustin asked about Carly and said he couldn't wait to see her again. They were cautioned not to say anything, except an ancestor of theirs' collected these articles and they found them recently.

They marched downstairs in groups. Dad took Pa, Josh, Bee and

Kelly first. They went down with everything hidden as Shawn originally found it. It looked like a tidy but ordinary basement. Shawn opened the first door and exposed the tunnel to the room full of artifacts. He reported that this was how he found them. "The museum had made copies, which we were now looking at."

Dad informed, "I have photos, you can see they are identical to what is hear. I would let you look closer at these, but we have people waiting."

They followed to another hidden room.

"What is this? Did someone live down here?" Bee asked.

"Yes, it was a young Jewish family. The man and wife and child lived here for months," answered Dad.

Everyone took time to look around at the bare necessities. The suit case, the simple old primitive bed and more. It was a damp eerie feeling as one imagined people living down here would feel the same. They walked through another tunnel to where the family died. The replicas of the dressed skeletons were still huddled as Shawn and Nerissa originally saw them. Pa cried at the sight and couldn't stop his tears.

You couldn't put yourself in their shoes without being crushed. Bee was sad at seeing the little sweater and red shoes still on the baby skeleton. "This was so awful," thought Josh.

They left in a melancholy mood and arrived upstairs, wiping their tears.

Everyone looked surprised at their sadness. Dad called the next group down stairs. This time Mac, Mark and Mom would go down. They were busy talking and kidding around when Dad opened the first door.

"Wow," said Mark.

They didn't expect to see so many more tunnel gadgets here, so far from Niagara. They were in awe of the artifacts and couldn't believe someone saved all this stuff and furthermore, died for it. It was so awesome and valuable. Mark was beside himself. They moved on to the other room. Dad told Mark this is where he found the picture of Mark's ancestor. He was the one that hid the Jewish people. The tears were already running down Mark's face. Mark tried to imagine his ancestor maybe helping to dig these tunnels and helping his friend gather these precious souvenirs of the past, hiding all the valuables, not knowing when they would be caught. He wished he could have known this courageous man. Mac was in bad shape too. Slowly holding hands for support, they walked to the little tunnel where the skeletons were. This family chose to die here, rather than give these artifacts over and reveal this tunnel to the Germans.

Mac and Mark hugged as they came out of what they called, "the death walk." Mark was beginning to realize his extravagant heritage and appreciated who he was for the first time.

After much thought they went upstairs and sent down Angela, Barry and Vanessa. By this time, they wondered what went on downstairs. Shawn showed them the ordinary basement and when Barry wasn't looking, opened the door. They followed Shawn in and he explained this was just the way they had found it. These artifacts were saved by giving someone's life for them. The boys upstairs never got a chance to know their great grandfather because of these artifacts. This house has been in the family for that long, except during the war when the Germans took it over for a short time. They did not find the tunnels and artifacts. We only found them when we were here last visit.

 Barry questioned, "How did you know to look here?"

"I cannot tell you, that it is privileged information," replied Dad.

They went on and saw the next room. Barry looked closely at the artifacts left behind. It was sad to think a little child was hidden here. Dad showed them into the tunnel of death. Vanessa was almost sick and Angela so shocked she could not speak. Barry understood the sacrifice that was in front of him. Shawn explained they chose death in the small cave instead of giving the hidden artifacts over to the Germans. Shawn let him know the outdoors was just a push away.

While waiting upstairs, Barry had noticed some pictures on the walls and one that looked just like Mark. "How was this possible," thought Barry?

"Are these men family?" he asked.

 Mary told Barry this was her relative and the other man in the photo looked like Mark. Barry asked who the other man was and Mary said it was Joseph Schultz, a friend of Mitchell Schwartz 1. Barry expressed that Mark looked just like this Joseph. Mary thought so too. That was all that was said, but Barry surmised there was more to this trip than he knew.

Next, they went to the, "Dimension of Time and Reality," a new museum. It would be amazing to take in after seeing the real thing. Mary and the boys came too. It was a solemn ride but the boys were excited for their guests to see it. The group had no idea what they were in for. We would be the first to view the displays and critique this new facility.

Pa and Shawn led the way with Mitchell and Dustin. It was a self-guided tour type of place, designed to promote thought and meditation. Pa was astounded how much this museum looked like the real location under the house. The letter written by Mitchell Schwartz I, was heard audibly as you looked at the artifacts he had gathered and saved. His passion was heard as you listened, while admiring these rescued treasures. You could pick the language of your choice. Mitchell and Dustin wiped their eyes and said they could not listen to the ancestor without fighting their emotions. Everyone felt the same way as they filed by and touched the reality of what once was. In the room where the Jewish family hid and then died, the words of Bernhardt Eisenhouwer pierced your soul, as you imagined living there with a small child and imagined the pain they must have felt to realize there was no future.

It looked like a gripping display from a time that should not be forgotten nor repeated.

The room where you wore gloves and could read the originals was extraordinary. Pa could have stayed for a longer time reading but we had a time-line to follow. The paintings were exquisite as we took time to look at every detail. I wondered what about these paintings made the Nazi Regime want to destroy them.

Everyone came out of that museum with a new appreciation for freedom of every kind, and life itself.

We said goodbye to the boys and Mary, acknowledging that they would be in Canada soon and we would look forward to the trio's arrival.

Barry expressed how emotional the day had been. He was not usually so touched as his job required some control, but he wasn't ready for this kind of revelation.

Shawn told the group they were going to a small town named Buelstedt. It was just an hour from Hamburg. They would experience a beautiful scenic ride. He assured them it was not going to be as interesting as the last and they would meet at an old cemetery. Everyone wanted to go again and Shawn was surprised. He did not want to occupy everyone's time, as it was their holiday too.

They drove out of town to the little town of Buelstedt. After taking a drive through the small village, they drove out to the cemetery. Carmela and Hannah Pilzer met them at the cemetery. They both looked well. The group paid their respects to the late Omie Pilzer. The kids noticed a gravestone of significance, bearing the name Carmelita Fry. They took pictures of it and Barry wondered why it was significant and again, what did he not know. Barry was becoming more and more curious regarding some of these questions he had.

They had a coffee at a coffee shop and said good-bye to Carmela and her granddaughter, Hannah. The rest of the day was spent taking a city tour of Hamburg. It was a beautiful old city with charming old buildings. Everyone had a slouch day. They did what they wanted. Shawn and the family took a hop-on hop-off combination cruise tour. The others took a hop-on hop-off city tour. It was a fun family day for them all. Mac and Mark came back with some neat souvenirs they were excited about. Pa and I witnessed a pickpocket in action. He was stealing a wallet and we helped to stop the man. He dropped the wallet and jumped off of the boat. The tourist was so grateful to get his identification and money back.

"Oh, I knew we should have tagged along with you, Josh. Something always happens!" said Mark.

"You live an exciting life, and something always happens when you are around!" added Mac and seconded by Mark.

They had a wonderful evening together and even took the time to play some games. It was ladies against the men. The women won as a result of stretching the truth. Everyone was packed for the next day as they were getting the train to Venice in the morning. The rental cars were left across the street from the train station before they boarded at six in the morning. The train ride into Venice would take sixteen hours. Everyone was looking forward to the gondolas that would be waiting to give the group a ride to our hotel. We would stay near the Marco Polo Square this time. Nerissa hoped she would have a coffee at her favorite restaurant again.

The gondolas were waiting at the canal for the group. It was Fritz, Stephan and Mel, all with gondolas. Shawn introduced Barry, Vanessa, and Angela to Mel and they were off. Fritz helped Bee, Mac, Kelly, Mark and Josh board his gondola. Shawn and Nerissa were in Stephan's gondola and were serenaded. He proved to have an awesome voice. Once again, they were on the canals of Venice! Everyone was in awe of their surroundings as it was night and the light romanticized the city even more than the newcomers could have imagined. Bee and Kelly took a moment to stand and just take in the sights after they disembarked and retrieved their luggage. They did not want to miss a thing. Angela was amazed that she was in Venice. Mac caught a glimpse of her dad kissing her mom and made a comment of disapproval. They laughed and wondered what it was that made Venice so romantic. They decided it was all the lights glimmering on the water.

Dad tried to pay the gondoliers, but of course, they would not take the money. They were happy to be of service, especially after what Nerissa and Shawn did for Fritz. They would check in with the group tomorrow and show them around the town. Everyone was ecstatic and could not wait.

The elevator was tiny to say the least. It led to a small hall with four doors. The first room was for Mac and her family. The second was for Mark and his mother. The third was for Pa, Kelly and Josh. The last room was for Shawn, Nerissa and Bee. It was a private elevator for just these rooms. How convenient was that? The rooms were in the style of Venice. Hand-blown glass light fixtures, ornate silk bedding and drapes with tassels. Even the walls were covered in silk to look like wall paper. The furniture was a painted antique finish, very prevalent in Venice. The windows had iron window boxes with potted flowers in them. Some overlooked the canals and others the gardens below.

After breakfast, the group was off to see Venice! It took two gondolas and Mel and Fritz were their chauffeurs. They gave them the longest and best tour anyone ever had of Venice. They stopped at Fritz's home and he showed them around the old building. Everyone was intrigued as it was so different from anything they had ever seen before. The old gondola was amazing! It was a beautiful piece of old-world craftsmanship. The water slips under the house were definitely unique to Venice's past and an interesting way of building. Stephan was working days and after he arrived home, they would go out for something to eat. Meanwhile, the group walked along the narrow pathways and bridges back into town. There was so much to see. The Grand Canal was not only awesome from the water, but also spectacular to view from the walkways and restaurants beside the wide waterway.

They had such a good time enjoying the sights and sounds of Venice! Mel arranged, with a friend of his, for the group to have a boat ride to the islands outside of the city. He would show them where the hand-blown glass was made on Murano Island. It would be another warm and interesting day on the waterways of Venice!

That evening, everyone went out on their own to enjoy Venice as they pleased. The teens went out with Fritz that evening. Bee and Kelly took a nice long walk to absorb as many memories as possible. Kelly bought Bee a lovely Murano glass Christmas ornament in a glass shop just off of the Grand Canal. They would hang it on their first Christmas tree together this year. They could hardly believe the wedding was just around the corner. Carly would be the maid of honor and Josh their best man. Mac and Mark would be attendants. The more they talked about the wedding the more excited they got. Kelly hoped his family would be able to make it, as they had livestock to feed. He understood their ways and priorities but would miss them. There was so much to think about and their minds were with the wedding even here in Venice.

They were going back the next day. It was such a treat to see the Friezen descendants doing so well and experiencing Venice with Bee's family and her friends. Too soon, the time of relaxation was over. Mary, Mitchell and Dustin would be moving in with Angela and Mark in a few weeks. The wedding preparations needed to be finished, and Shawn and Pa were preoccupied, seeming to have something else up their sleeves.

CHAPTER 27

Barry Discovers

They were into the everyday life at home and enjoying every minute of it. Mom and Bee were busy getting every detail ready for the wedding. They only had a couple of months to go before the big day. The gazebo was ready, thanks to Grammpy, and so was the yard. They couldn't think of another thing to do to the house. Grammy had done so much baking and cooking for the occasion. It was a good thing they owned an oversized freezer. Nerissa was sure they would need it all.

Dad spent a bit of time in the tunnels with Pa and Josh. They were always carrying something down below. What were they doing?

They scheduled the company from Europe and South America to arrive a week before the wedding. That first weekend, Pa would host a dinner party at the Angel Inn Restaurant, as that was where they were all staying. It was right in town and convenient for the guests. They would provide a van for their guests to use, and to do some touring of the area.

Dad, Pa and Josh were ready for the secret event. The time was passing quickly and the end of summer nearing. Where did the last couple of months go?

Now they could help the ladies with the wedding as their minds were put at ease regarding the tunnels. The guests would arrive by airbus on their own schedule, and we sent whoever was able and free at the time to greet them. Pa, Mac and Mark greeted Lauren and Joel. The younger two siblings, Manny and Adam, had to stay behind because of commitments to school. Manny was working towards a scholarship and so decided to keep Adam with him since it was such a long tiring flight for the youngster. They would be missed by the Canadian family as they knew how much Manny dreamed of coming to Canada. He would come another time. Josh and Pa greeted Fritz and Stephan. Shawn and Nerissa went to greet Carmela and Hannah. They had all arrived and were settled at the Inn.

Tomorrow night would be the memorial service. The guests had no idea what was to come. They would all be introduced to each other before dinner in the Inn. The prime rib was a specialty and everyone would enjoy it. The Inn's age and history was the perfect location for this occasion.

Today there were still many things to do. Shawn was checking out something to do with the lights in the gazebo when he heard a noise underneath it. Who could be down there? The family was all working on the yard and the wedding today, including Angela and Mark. Could it be Mac? Shawn quietly snuck around the stairs of the gazebo and saw the boards were moved. He looked in and was shocked.

"Barry, what are you doing down here?" he asked, climbing into the space.

"I knew things around here didn't add up. How about you tell me what is going on?"

"What do you mean?" Shawn shot back.

Barry was carrying a flashlight and announced, "With the tunnel, Shawn. What did you think I was talking about?"

"Have you been down there?" Shawn half whispered.

"Yes," he announced. "But just part of the way."

Shawn asked if they could go back down and said he would show him something. Shawn led the way and Barry followed. Shawn took Barry down to the storage room and then to the underground living room. He told him the story of Vinnie killing Omz and trying to kill Bee, Mark, and Mac.

"What? I did not know that! You should have told me that; I am her father!" he said angrily.

Shawn understood totally but continued as there was so much to tell. "Pa hid in the tunnels because he was trying to save his family.

Josh and I hid in the tunnel as Vinnie and his accomplice, Nick named "The Suit", came after us. The two criminals followed Mac into the tunnels as she was running for her life. The killers ran off the edge, but not until one met the cougar. The cougar was friendly as long as he recognized your scent. We found out why the tunnels were built from plans Pa found. They found gold and coins and had the money in American and European bank accounts. Most importantly we found the wills of those Germans who died in the tunnels during the war. Barry the people you met in Europe were ancestors of the prisoners who built and died in these tunnels. Jervaih and Lovlyn were squatters who we found on the families homestead in Germany. Pa and I did research to find the descendants of the wills we found in the tunnels. It was our aim to right the wrongs of the past and honor the men that sacrificed their lives. By the way, Mac and Josh were the first to discover the tunnels a couple of years ago. Pa, of course, knew of them for years and had done research on why they were here and who built them. Mac and Josh found most of the evidence of what happened in these tunnels. We meaning, the kids including Mac and Mark, have done quite an extensive search through them all the way to the hydro-electric plant. Barry, you have got to believe me, we have done nothing wrong. It is our property and we were checking it out! We know we might have to prove all of this to you and we will, but I have no time before the wedding. There are bones of the ancestors of the guests from Europe and South America down there and we have not touched them out of respect. We have been careful to document everything with photos before we touched or disturbed it. We even found out that two Nazi soldiers befriended the German prisoners and gave their lives for the captives. One German prisoner left his money to one of the German soldier's family. We assume the other had no family, as some would have been left to him as well. The prisoners seemed to be very conscientious and particular about dividing up the money equally. Mac can show you and Vanessa around after the wedding if you like. She knows these tunnels as well as anyone. The tunnels go to the house and down from the Carriage house. The only ones that know about this are you, Mac, Mark, and our family, including Kelly. It is imperative that no one think there is gold to find and that our family is not put into danger again," Dad was finally done talking.

Barry shook his head and didn't know what to say. Of course, he had many questions and would wait to ask them later. That much he could do.

"How did you think to look under the gazebo?" Shawn asked.

"When Mac was ill, with a high temperature, she started to talk. She talked about tunnels, and the gazebo with someone after her, and a friendly cougar.

"I am very sorry we had to keep this from you. We did the best we could with what we knew, and after all of our hard work, it finally paid off. I will need some help tomorrow if you can bring yourself to help me?"

"What do you need? And don't think that we won't talk about this some more!" he assured.

"That will be my pleasure, but for now, do not tell a soul, as I want a peaceful and safe wedding for Bee, please! Grammy and Grammpy also know. Did I tell you that? I have forgotten, as I was talking a hundred miles an hour."

"You were going to tell me something I could help with?" Barry asked.

Shawn told Barry how he could help and showed him the tunnel to the carriage house garage exit. They passed the opening where the sacks lay, and where the men climbed a rope to their death. Barry couldn't believe the cold-heartedness of the Germans. Barry was shown how to open the secret door from the tunnel side and the garage side. Shawn knew Angela and Mary were helping Nerissa in the mansion and he and Barry were alone. Barry and Vanessa would join the group for dinner the next night. Mac would be so happy that she did not have to make up stories for her mom and dad anymore.

"Barry, this is a secret only Pa, Josh, I ,and now you of course know about. This surprise is for the descendants, my family, as well as Mac and now her family. You can let Vanessa come and be surprised."

Barry agreed to do the job he was given. He was still amazed that all these secrets lay beneath the property next to his. He would have to check out the dynamite cleanup, even though it was not publicized.

He needed to know the homes and gorge were not in any danger. Of course, he would do this anonymously.

CHAPTER 28

Pa's Identity

Pa stood in front of the fireplace, looking down at the floor. He had never noticed this before. Nerissa had moved a small carpet to have it cleaned. One board had been nailed down like the one at the homestead. He bent to have a good look. Mom came in and asked if he was alright.

"I would like to take this floor board off if you don't mind, Nerissa. I will put it back."

Nerissa went to get her small toolbox and came back with a hammer. Pa worked at the nails and pulled them up. The boards lifted and he peered in. There was an old box! He took it out and recognized his mother's handwriting.

Pa translated it, "To our dear son, Harry. We have finally been able to adopt you, without suspicion cast on you regarding who you are. We pray you have had a good life with us as we have been blessed to have raised you as our own. Here are the adoption papers. We are so sorry, as we never found just the right time to tell you about the adoption. Your loving mother and father."

"Well Dad, you know you were legally adopted! Pa was glad it was made legal. He thought of the implications of the family inheritance for Bee and Josh. He sat with his papers in hand and imagined the worry his mother and father endured. They knew he would be wanted and maybe even killed because of his true identity. He knew his parents did everything they could to protect their son. He was fine with all the decisions they had made to protect him. He felt sympathy for his biological mother who loved her unborn child and named him even before his birth. How honorable for his parents to keep the name. He had the most wonderful upbringing that anyone could have. He was able to pass down what was placed in his hands by his parents. He had given their legacy, as well as his, to not one, but two generations. Pa felt like their dreams had been fulfilled. He had dreams of his own and felt like a huge chunk was missing. Omz needed to be there to fill them in. It was still a dull ache even after all this time. He had gone on with his life and figured his time in the tunnels, hiding in lonely despair, were probably not the best ingredient for healing after Omz died. He felt his life would take a better turn from here on in. He was surrounded with so many people that loved and cared about him.

CHAPTER 29

The Guests Arrive

It was the next evening and all the guests were ready for dinner. It had been a busy day walking about the quaint old town of Niagara-on-the-Lake and enjoying the shops and the outstanding flowers. For the dinner, they were told to dress casual, have jackets and wear comfortable walking shoes. They assumed they would walk down town in the village or to the waterfront walkway where the gazebo stood. They were a large group.

After they gathered, they were asked if they were ready for an adventure. They all replied, "Yes, of course!"

First, they had their delicious meal, enjoying the atmosphere of the old inn and each other. By the time they were finished, they had formed a good rapport with one another. It was dark by now and time to put the plan into action. Pa drove Grammy, Grammpy, Josh, Bee, Kelly and Mom. Dad drove Carmela, Hannah, Mark, Angela and Mary. Barry drove Mac, Dustin, Mitchell and Lauren. Vanessa was recruited to drive Joel, Fritz, and Stephan.

We made sure we had vehicles rented with dark tinted windows. They drove for a while and the passengers were asked to put blindfolds on. It was all part of their night and they would not be sorry. While driving the occupants sat and chatted with blindfolds on, wondering about the game they were surprised with. Their curiosity was piqued. One of the cars slipped away from the rest, and sacks were given to the guests to put over their heads as well as the blindfolds.

They went along with it as their hosts had earned their trust and respect in doing so much for them. Pa's car was the first to drive into the carriage house garage and the door closed after them. Grammy, Grammpy, Kelly and Mom had no blindfolds on. Bee and Josh did, as they were the last descendants of the prisoners. They all entered the tunnel and Bee and Josh were led down some stairs and told to wait. They, of course, figured out where they were by the feel of the wall, but liked the intrigue of the game. Pa pulled his car out of the garage and parked it on the yard between the river and the mansion and joined the others. Then Vanessa brought her car into the garage and it closed. Her guests gladly wore their sacks over their heads and played the game. Joel, Fritz and Stephan were led down the stairs a little ways and Vanessa stayed with them. Pa pulled her car out and parked it with the first one. Barry was next with his group who already had their sacks over their heads. He pulled into the garage and closed the door. His passengers got out. Mac, Dustin, Mitchell and Lauren were next to be led down the stairs to wait with Barry. Mac knew where she was as she felt the walls, and she recognized the familiar smell. She did not say a word. It felt eerie coming in this way with no flashlight and no lantern, as far they could tell. The car was taken care of and Shawn drove in. Carmela, Hannah, Mark, Angela, and Mary had their sacks over their heads. Dad closed the garage door. The passengers were unloaded and carefully led down the stairs. For now, they were chuckling at what this game was as they were carefully taken down some more steps. They were told to take off their sacks and blindfolds. The lights were out when they bared their eyes. Even while open they could not see hands in front of their eyes. You could hear sounds of shock and fear amongst the guests. Dad had their attention

He started, "This is where your ancestors were brought against their will, as captives. Remember the feeling when you took your blindfolds off, although you thought it was a game. They had traveled far, being frightened and mistreated. Arriving somewhere that they would never see is unimaginable to us. They were smuggled into the country. Once here, they stood where you stood, not knowing how they got here. They were divided into different groups to be commanded by soldiers. The guards that had access to the outside stayed in this area and higher. The prisoners were taken down to somewhere, they didn't know where, to be kept separated."

Dad turned on his lantern. Pa, Barry, and Mom gave everyone a flashlight to turn on, making sure they knew their ancestors would have followed a soldier with a lantern. They all passed by the opening in the tunnel, where their ancestors had to climb down the ropes, before they were killed. Dad had them leave their blindfolds and sacks at that place without telling them of this history.

"Notice the opening in the wall and the pile of sacks," he made known.

Everyone took note and was puzzled. We took our time, as we had seniors with us, and there was no rush. Everyone was intrigued with the long rock tunnel leading downward. We had finally arrived to the lake cavern. The group slid through to the little cave where we found Pa. Then they were directed to the tunnel that they would crawl through. Now, Grammy knew why we insisted she wear a pair of slacks even though this was foreign to her. Dad showed everyone the wooden planks that we had put into place. These made their access to the next tunnel possible. He let them know of the deep endless hole in the floor beneath them. They straightened their backs and were glad to be through and standing again. Dad led the way.

"It will be quite a descent so take your time," Dad warned.

As they descended Dad pointed out the holes cut into the rock walls. When they got to the bottom, everyone was facing away from the skeletons as Dad directed their attention upward. Earlier, Barry was told to stay behind. Pa gave a eulogy on his uncle, Friedrich Wittfoot. This was not a report on the date of birth or death as much as the way of his faith and life.

Dad continued, "Friedrich and Daniel suddenly disappeared in Germany during the war. Herbert, the other brother, moved to Canada with his son and wife, not knowing what happened to his brothers. I want to light an opening for him as a memorial as you listen to his last words and testament, written in his own handwriting, found in one of these tunnels."

Barry lit a lantern and hung it in the first high opening in the wall as Friedrich's words echoed in the hollow cavern, the way Pa had recorded them,

> *"My name is Friedrich Wittfoot.*
> *I am in captivity.*
> *My brother is Herbert Wittfoot.*
> *My brother Daniel died in prison in Germany.*
> *I secretly hid my money.*
> *Please give the money to my brother Herbert and his son.*
> *I have been here for five years.*
> *My God has helped me this far and I will see him soon."*

Everyone was solemn and didn't quite know what to make of it.

Dad continued and said he wanted to the light the second light for Joseph Schultz.

The voice sounded through the cave as the recording played. Joseph, already in his 50s, had a son by a woman before he was married and supported the child while in Germany. He married in his 60s and his much younger wife knew of his son. She agreed in supporting the child and that the two should stay in touch. During captivity, he secretly sent a letter out to his son, telling him about the money he was receiving. He hoped the letter wasn't confiscated and that his son received it. His son was asked to share the news and money with Joseph's daughter. She was born just before Joseph was imprisoned. Vinnie, his son, became obsessed with finding this money, to the point of becoming willing to kill people to find it. He killed Omz, tried to kill Mark, Bee, and Mac as well as Bella. In total contradiction to what Joseph was all about, one of his offspring became greedy and evil. It is a warning to us to make the right choices and become aware, like Joseph, who saved lives during the war, hiding Jewish people underground.

Although Vinnie was ruthless, Joseph also had a daughter who was honorable and lived life as he would have. He would have been proud of her and her child.

Mark loved hearing about his grandfather, Joseph. It made him proud, and he wanted to be just like him.

Dad spoke again and declared another light to be lit in honor of Mitchell Schwartz I. He added that they would hear the words of Mr. Schwartz translated in English. His granddaughter-in-law, Mary, still owned the family home that Mr. Schwartz had resided in. Not so long ago, many artifacts, books, paintings and such were found in this house. His will was also found here in the tunnel, and this letter was found in his home in Germany.

The haunting words sounded,

> *"Dear loved ones. If you find this letter, it must mean that the enemy has taken me, or my loved ones have found this secret. I pray it will be my family. I hid books and art upstairs as a deterrent. The basement also secretly housed boxes of books, art, and other treasures, as well as old dishes. I saved these special artifacts and gave my life for them so future generations could enjoy and appreciate them. I hope they are still in good condition upon finding by you. I am giving these to the last generation alive, hoping you are living in freedom and God's blessings. The cavern and tunnel were dug with my own hands and I carried the earth to the back yard at night. My good friend helped when he could. This was before the war. God gave me a sense of things to come and I obeyed, not knowing what the room would be used for. The work was done while my wife was away for the summer visiting her family. When she returned, I just had to explain the dirt mound and garden on top of it. I couldn't explain, and asked her to trust me and she did. God blessed me with a good woman. When the war broke out, I tried my best to fill this room with valuables for the future. May this generation love them as much as I do?*
>
> *Go with God before you,*
> *Mitchell Schwartz."*

Everyone was very shocked at the connection to the tunnels and Germany and direct proof in both places.

Dad continued, "There was something else found at the same home. We found pictures of Mitchell I with Joseph Schultz. Appar-

ently, they were good friends. There was another surprise in the basement in another room and tunnel. It was a hiding place, and we found
a family of skeletons sitting near an exit. Listen to words of Mr. Bernhardt Eisenhouwer, who sacrifice himself and his family,

> *"Committed friends,*
>
> *I, Mr. Eisenhouwer, have written this as a last testament
> of my family's life here on this earth. We were hidden by our
> friend, Joseph, at the home of Mitchell Schwartz. The latter
> man has fed and hidden us for six months. We are so grate-
> ful for both of their sacrifices for us. My wife, Ramona, and
> our little girl, Natasha, are both very ill and dying. There is
> no more food being delivered and we are out of water. I tried
> to dig our way out the back way as we had been directed, but
> the soldiers were camped right beside the hill. Mitchell told
> me a human life is more important to save than art, and that
> my family and I were a priority. This is true, but we chose to
> stay in the tunnel and not disclose ourselves, or the art, to the
> enemy, as we know we would have been shot instantly. We
> pray generations to come will experience the freedom to enjoy
> all that is hidden here."*

The group was very quiet as they were coming to grips with the
magnitude of the war, and its pain. You could hear the sniffling and
see the shadows of the tissues wiping these good people's eyes.

Dad had another light lit for Mr. Fry. "Mr. Fry was a prisoner in
the tunnels, as valuable a man as all the rest. We know nothing else
about him but that he gave his money to his descendants. We know he
worked hard or would have been killed and replaced."

Five more lights were lit for the Ritmeir brothers. They witnessed
the murder of everyone in their family by firing squad. They were tak-
en as prisoners and then here to the tunnels. The brothers had no
remaining relatives and designated their wage to be split amongst the
prisoners. We grieve their loss of family and the loss of time to live as
human beings improving the world. We also found their money and
gold here in the tunnels.

Dad asked for another light to be lit.

"This light is to honor Mr. Stephan Friezen. He worked and died in these tunnels. Thinking of his family before he died, he left his money to them. You are standing in the midst of his contribution to the project, that he was forced to create, not ever knowing where he was."

Dad ordered another two lights to be lit and spoke. "We honor the Kempt Brothers who also toiled here in the tunnels. This is the letter translated for you. It was written on the back of an order form to kill all the prisoners. The light will also give honor to a soldier, who chose compassion and righteousness before duty and orders."

The words started,

"The soldier did not obey orders to kill us. He was killed by his commanding officer when it was discovered that we were still alive. The gold was left just before the tunnel to the top, where we were going to be taken in the morning to die. We were interrupted from putting the gold under the rubble. We did not believe our lives would be spared and knew the end was imminent. The guards were rounding up all the prisoners into one area for the night. This soldier was to guard us. He helped us collect all the maps and gave them to Friedrich Wittfoot, who would hide them. Friedrich knew how to get into all the passages, tunnels and rooms, as he was one of the masterminds. The soldier assisted in covering for us as we hid our money. The five Ritmeir brothers had no remaining family, as they witnessed their murder by firing squad before being taken to prison. I have a wife and two sons. My brother is not married and has no children. The soldier's family should get my brother Rudy Kempt's share, as Rudy specified. The soldier's name is Herman Wolfgang. He has a wife and family. We found his body in the tunnel and gave him a quick burial under the rocks. It was the best we could do under the circumstances.

Tell my family I love them, Eckhart Kempt."

Dad spoke encouragingly, "These men left a legacy of good deeds in caring for each other and their families under the most horrifying circumstances. I want to mention one more person. That is a German soldier, Helmut. We found a picture of him in South America with Herman and it stated they were going to be sent on a secret mission.

"This is what we found, left by Helmut in these tunnels."

Pa translated the first piece of paper from German to English and recorded it.

It was a document sent as an order to kill the prisoners within a day. The guards could take their money as payment for a job successfully done. There was to be no evidence of the prisoners and money. The second piece of paper was a hand written letter from all the prisoners with their names on it.

It stated,

"This soldier would try to get out by another exit. He was given one bar of gold from each prisoner. He promised to give it to their families as soon as possible. This soldier, as well as one other, had become friends after spending so much time in these tunnels with us. This was why we had such good fellowship with each other. They made it possible. They were also blindfolded and did not know where we were located. They got their orders from soldiers stationed part of the way up the tunnel. The two soldiers were kept here with us the whole time, prisoners themselves, but making our lives much improved. We know we are going up to die tomorrow and these men have decided to help us. One was helping us hide our wills and this soldier was given a brick of gold from each of us, for our families. The Ritmeir brothers, not having any living family, decided to give their gold to the other prisoners, now their only family. This soldier volunteered to give his life for our cause. He said he did not know how long he had left, as he was already coughing up blood. He would gather the twelve gold bars into the small cave near a place that he could escape from, and blow the rock away. We gathered sacks so he could cover himself and wait for the day when no one was around."

"These two soldiers wanted nothing for themselves, only to help the prisoners reach their families with financial aid. They defied their orders and chose a humanitarian response. None of these prisoners would have lived as long as they did, if not treated well by these two guards. We honor them today."

As the glow of the flickering lights made a captivating dance on the irregular stone cavern walls, the group seemed entranced. The lights created a warmth on the otherwise cold hard rock surface. Dad spoke softly and asked the group to turn and shine their lights toward him as he moved to the skeletal monument. They all gasped! Dad reported that most of these bones were left just as they had been found. They wanted to identify as many as possible. Friedrich was identified because of his missing fingers. The soldiers' skeletons lay in a bit of disorder and Dad apologized, as their remains were moved from elsewhere and difficult to retrieve. Joseph Schultz was identified because they found a photo and it showed two gold teeth one on each side.

Mark was in awe and had to ask, "Where is he?"

Pa took him around the back and there was a skull with nice straight teeth and two were gold. Mark got emotional at the sight of his grandfather, more than he ever thought he would. After hugging his mom, he actually bent over and with a loving gesture touched the skull. His dream of finding his ancestor was realized. He almost couldn't stop crying, until his mom came and gave him another hug.

Dad spoke more regarding the soldier. "This soldier is your ancestor, Lauren and Joel. His relatives, being you, were given Rudy Kempt's share of the money."

Lauren and Joel were so taken back that he was such a good man, and they had been so ashamed of having a German soldier for their ancestor. It was life changing to have this kind of person to pattern their lives after. They were so humbled to know of this righteous man. They hugged each other acknowledging their pride in their ancestor.

Pa asked if anyone else had any generational markings that could be traced by a skeleton.

Fritz almost shouted, "Yes, I have, or used to have an extra small toe, until they operated. So did my dad! Maybe…?"

We all took our flashlights and checked the skeletal feet. We were on our knees crawling and bending low. This was a difficult and tedious task.

"There it is!" announced Lauren. "If you look way in there, you can see it."

Fritz and his father studied it and yes, there was an extra bone beside the small toe. "This is our relative!" they said with joy. To actually see the person's remains was monumental. Fritz and Stephan were beside themselves, "Dad, this is really our relative!" said Fritz.

Dad again reminded everyone that he already had the proof that they were all the ancestors of these remains. This exercise was just so they could bury the ancestors with dignity as well as this group's permission. Joel contemplatively asked if anyone thought the bodies should stay just as they were, all together, just as they died. If they were buried somewhere else, people would ask questions. It made sense and Dad thought we could have a vote on it.

"Raise your hands if you want the grave to stay as it is," Dad asked.

Everyone raised their hands. "It is decided, we will leave things the way they are," Dad said.

Dad continued, "After you pay your respects, we will make our way back upstairs. First, I would like you to look up again, way up, to the highest light."

Barry had put a couple of lights into the opening from where the men fell.

"That is the point where the men had to climb through an opening, out onto a ledge, and then climb down the ropes. The ropes were put on fire, and the men fell to their death. That is why pieces of burnt rope lay amongst the skeletons."

The group was appalled at the idea of men doing this to one another, and Dad reiterated that we had to be careful what master we served. One could be very cruel and heartless and the other kind and compassionate.

CHAPTER 30

The Inheritance

After telling the group they would not see this place again, because it was too dangerous, they were told that they now had time to look around.

Pa stepped up and said some kind words to the guests. He ended with saying a blessing over all the descendants of those who died here. He declared wisdom over the decisions they would be making for their families now and in the future. With those words they started the journey back.

The group slowly made their way to the top, looking through the lit openings as they made their way up the stairs. When they arrived to where the men fell to their death, Dad stopped them all. They all had a chance to look through the opening down into the tomb.

"We are almost back now. In a minute, we will need you to put your blindfolds back on and the sacks over your heads. The reason we are doing this is so you understand how helpless these men were and so you can feel just a minuscule portion of their plight. Also, it is being done for the protection of everyone here. If word got out of this place, everyone's life would be in danger. Rumors of gold drive people to do things unimaginable. Do you understand why this secret has to be kept? Thank you, everyone, for being the kind of people that your ancestors would have been proud of. You made the next step possible."

Everyone was in agreement to keep this a secret. They knew from the past murder of Omz, and attempts on the other lives, that it was crucial.

"I have in my possession, money in the form of a cheque. It was designated to every one of you by your family member. I saved one of my bars of gold, so you could see and feel it for yourselves. Feel how heavy it is."

He held it out and passed it around, so everyone got a chance to feel and see it. He gave them all one of the coins, made into a necklace on a chain, as a remembrance. They placed them around their necks with reverence.

"I am pleased to give you your inheritance. We cashed in the gold and the coins anonymously, and put them into a foreign bank account." Dad passed the cheques out with the help of Pa. They all got over one million and seven hundred thousand dollars. They were totally stunned.

"My children's inheritance will be the same as yours when this bar of gold is added."

"I would like to give something to someone who has asked for nothing and kept this secret for safety sake, even jeopardizing her life. Without her and Josh, none of us would be standing here. Mac, this is for you."

She couldn't believe that she heard her name; she was getting an inheritance too. Mac felt awkward and overwhelmed as she felt she did not deserve this. Dad coached that she could use it for her education or her future, or however she wanted. Our family wanted her to have it, and no one would have their money if it wasn't for her. She was so grateful and said she would use it wisely as she knew what the men in the tunnels went through for it. Mac hugged Dad and Pa and said thank you again.

"It almost makes me feel like I have an inheritance from one of my... ancestors!" she announced. "I feel like I know them all so well."

Dad added, "Mac, these men gave all those that deserved the money an equal share. We saw that when they rewarded the soldiers."

"I told you, Mac, you can share my relatives, no problem!" Josh spoke to break the awkwardness Mac felt.

Everyone looked at their cheques as Dad ordered, and were astounded. They each received almost two million dollars! There were tears, smiles, hugs and just silent moments. Pa couldn't believe their task of giving to the ancestors was over. It had been a long time since he had found the tunnels. If only Omz didn't have to die. He would give it all up to have her back. He knew he would have to be brave and look forward to the future. He had so much to be thankful for.

Dad reminded them to put the cheques away before the blind-folds were put on. They were all led out the same way from that point, one car at a time. We would all meet back at the Angel Inn for some refreshments and conversation. The private room was set up with coffee tea and snacks. Everyone could speak freely as we would be alone. One thing that was mentioned a few times, was that they would not change their lives but be able to pay their bills. That would be change enough. No one would know by their life styles. They asked if they could have a reunion in a year. Dad thought we could discuss that later on. Someone else suggested the reunion be in a different location, in their different countries. They were all great ideas and the group seemed well connected. They would stay in town for the wedding and get to know each other even better.

They talked about how it felt to be blindfolded, totally at someone else's mercy. It was scary being in the dark not knowing if they could move without getting hurt. The picture of the cavern with the flickering lights was one that was burnt into their memory. It left them in awe. They said they would never forget it, as well as the words they heard resounding in the cave from their ancestors. The most shocking experience was the mound of skeletal remains. It was not expected and it was a horrific picture of war crimes. No one could forget that.

Mark was so ecstatic and couldn't stop talking about Joseph. It was like Joseph was a part of his present life. He was in awe of having Joseph with him, even if only a skeleton. It was tangible and not to be denied. Angela couldn't quite get her head around all she had learned this night. Her father was such an outstanding man. She never realized as that part of his life was never spoken of.

Barry thanked Shawn for his kindness in sharing with Mac. He now understood why Shawn was able to pay for the trip to Europe and South America. Barry let him know that Shawn and Pa and the kids had done an outstanding job in research and discovering the clues to the gold and coins. Mac was so excited to take them down to the tunnels and show her parents around one day.

Pa told Josh that a big weight had been lifted off his shoulders. He felt so good about the memorial service and fulfilling the wishes of the dead. He felt like he could start living life again and thought he would give Bella and Andy a little money in honor of Omz. After all, she was going to help this girl get on her feet. Josh agreed, and knew Bella would welcome some financial help. Barry had relayed that Bella and Andy would have to find new living arrangements for the winter, as the trailer was not heated.

Kelly expressed how grateful he was to have experienced this evening with the family. It was a big part of their lives and he loved sharing it with Bee. It was something he had never experienced, and knew he would never forget how moving it was. It made him think of his family heritage and how he should cherish their habits and customs with a new sense of quality for life, appreciating them for their sacrifices. He was learning so much, and knew life would teach him many more lessons. Everyone was so grateful for the kind generous man Dad was, and promised to reimburse him for the financial help he gave them.

CHAPTER 31

The Clock Tower

Kelly, Pa and Josh were going into Niagara-on-the-Lake to pick up some supplies. Pa wanted to go into the Tourist Information Centre in the basement of the Old Town Hall to get some information for the guests. It was downstairs in the basement of the old Court House. They walked down a little hall. Pa looked into a room that said, "Private."

"Should you be doing that Pa?" asked Kelly.

"Well, a few years back I was invited into this room and asked to check it out. My life changed direction and I never got a chance. Just thought since we were here..."

Josh jumped in with, "Yes Pa, let's do it!"

We followed Pa into a storage room. He looked around with the light on and closed the door tightly behind us.

"What are you looking for Pa? asked Josh.

"I'm not sure," he replied.

They were touching and lifting everything. There was not much in there except some papers and other office supplies, plus a bucket and mop for washing the floors. Pa took out the key chain flashlight and started to examine the wall closely. The mortar between the bricks of the wall seemed to be missing in a three by three section, making a square.

"I think I found something," whispered Pa. He pushed a small cabinet aside to reveal the whole area.

As he studied it further, he pushed on an area that seemed to recede more than the other. The small opening appeared as the wall moved.

Josh was ready to enter when Kelly said, "Are you sure this is okay?"

Pa answered with a chuckle, "Well, we will never know until we have checked it out."

They moved in with only two flashlights and were shocked when the door closed behind them. Josh always carried a flashlight in his pocket like others carried a pocketknife. It's too bad he didn't have his exploration bag with him. They kept on going and the tunnel was now tall enough for them to stand in. It was made of cut brick, laid in an arched form.

"Pa, will this end up at the clock tower?" asked Josh.

"We will see, son," answered Pa.

Walking for quite some time Pa figured we were past the clock tower. Finally, we got to a wooden door. It was not a large, grand door, but simply made with old wide boards. Pa opened it as we held our breath. We were in a small room in a basement. We needed to know what building we were in.

"Let me go upstairs and try to find out what building we are in," Josh pleaded.

"Okay, be careful," Pa said, giving in.

Josh went into another room in the basement and went up the stairs. He cautiously opened the door. There were paintings on the walls. He recognized them. They were famous paintings. Everyone would recognize them. He was in an art gallery.

"Awesome I thought," sneaking back into the staircase. When I got to Pa and Kelly, and told them where I was, they were amazed.

Pa figured the tunnel had to have been used many years ago by the owner of the estate. Who knows for what? Maybe it was used for the underground railroad, or in the days of prohibition.

We decided to head back and made sure the door was locked properly behind them. I reminded Pa that no one would find this tunnel from the house, as the whole room was clad with the same rustic wood. We made sure to scour the walls of the tunnel with their small flashlights. I brushed against the wall as he walked and noticed something different with his light. I backed up and looked at it again.

"Look, Pa, it is another cut out in the bricks. Josh pushed it hard as the brick door moved. It took both Kelly and Josh to push it back. They entered another tunnel. It seemed quite short compared to the previous passage, as they neared another wooden door. Josh pushed it but it wouldn't open. He stuck his finger into a knothole and pulled at it. To his surprise, it opened easily. They moved back to open it all the way. There was a narrow set of stairs upward. Pa went first, carefully checking each step to see if it was still safe. The stairs turned into a ladder.

Pa whispered, "I know where we are!"

"Where?" Kelly asked.

"I know, we are in the Clock Tower, aren't we?" Josh asked.

"Let me climb back down and I will let you see what I am seeing," said Pa.

Kelly went first and had a look around. Josh then went up and was amazed. He could look all the way down Queen St.

"What a view." Kelly told Pa.

You could even see the water at the end of the street. When he looked out of a peep hole, the opposite way, he could see the park and hospital.

" You wouldn't miss a thing if you were looking for someone or something," Josh muttered as he took his turn.

Kelly could not believe that he had just assisted in finding a new tunnel. He enjoyed the thrill of the not knowing what was behind the next door or wall. Josh reminded Kelly that this area was full of undiscovered, as well as known tunnels. He would enjoy living around here. We got back to the basement of the tourism office and Pa picked up the pamphlets we needed. We left there looking like all the other tourists. We were wearing smiles on our faces because of our new secret. We had a close look at the Clock Tower from the outside, both front and back. Someone had done an awesome job in camouflaging the peep holes. Kelly couldn't wait to tell Bee what he had done today.

CHAPTER 32

The Wedding and More

The chairs were all in rows with an aisle down the middle. The chairs were dressed in white covers with large bows at the back. Bee wanted babies-breath tucked in the back of each chair.

The gazebo was adorned with white netting and a babies-breath swag under the roof line and along the hand rail. A new chandelier hung in the middle giving a soft glow. The day had finally arrived. The whole house porch rail was done in white netting and babies-breath. Small tables with white cloths and bud vases with one rose and a sprig of babies-breath finished the porch. There were five chairs to each table. Each chair was dressed in white. On the back porch, facing the river, the buffet table was placed. The bar was placed at the far end of the porch for the drinks. There were round tables through-out the yard. Each table had candles to enhance the ambiance. The dance floor at the edge of the property, overlooking the water, made a romantic vista. The trunk of the high tree was tightly wound with soft white lights. There were soft spot lights enhancing every area, and it screamed with romance in all directions. You could get a lovely breeze sitting near the dance floor while enjoying the music. Bee and Kelly had a live band with all of their favorite songs picked out.

The guests arrived and mingled with each other until the cere-mony started. The best man, Josh, and usher, Mark, made sure every-one was comfortable. Carly, the maid of honor was giving Dustin her full attention. He seemed to be in total awe of her. She looked radiant, and he was overwhelmed with her beauty as well as her personality. They were seeing a lot of each other and Bee could see another wedding in the future. Mac, her bridesmaid, looked stunningly sophisticated, a look that Josh and Mark were not used to seeing in her. She looked so adult as they paused to look at her, not realizing they were in the same category today. Grammy and Grammpy were chatting with everyone, making sure the hors d'oeuvres were served. Grammy had made them all herself. Pa mingled and chatted, enjoying the small talk, as he made his rounds.

Kelly looked over the guests and spotted his family. How nice it was to see them all here, even the youngest. His father's neighbor had volunteered to feed the livestock and take care of the farm. The amazing thing was that the neighbor was not Amish, but he wanted to make this special trip possible for the family. "They all look so wonderful in their new clothing," thought Kelly. His mom and sisters had the same color purple dresses, as that is what they were used to. They bought one bolt of material and used it for everyone. He was blessed with a wonderful heritage and appreciated and loved his family just as they were; plain.

Bee was getting dressed, assisted by Mom. She glowed in her dress and felt like a princess. Carly hurried in to assist in the preparation. Bee's long blonde hair was perfectly done to compliment her off the shoulder dress. She wore a medium length train that flowed from the back of her head and cascading curls. Her tall slim bride profile would have made the wedding magazines drool.

"Bee, you look so beautiful," Carly announced, with tears coming to her eyes.

After a warm embrace, they went on to the next task. Carly was sent to give Josh the cue to get the musicians in place near the gazebo and have them start to play. People would know to wander over to their seats near the gazebo and wait for the ceremony. The sun was going down and the lights were all lit. It was taking on a marvelously enchanting look. The spotlights behind the gazebo lit up trees on the hill and added to the mood. All the focus was on the gazebo.

Most of Kelly's family was seated and then the rest of Bee's family followed. All the guests had taken their seats and waited. Josh, Carly,

Mark, and Mac took their places in front of the gazebo. Pastor Bill waited patiently inside it. Kelly walked his parents down the aisle and kissed them before they sat down in the front row. Then Kelly stood in front of the gazebo waiting for his bride.

Mom and Dad walked Bee in and Dad gave her hand to Kelly. No one said anything, as the symbolism was clearly understood. Dad and Mom kissed Bee and hugged Kelly, then sat down. Kelly took Bee's hand and escorted her into the gazebo. The ceremony was simple and meaningful. They declared their love for each other in their own words. The rings were exchanged and the license was signed. Pastor Bill had just asked the bride and groom to kiss when they heard screaming. Everyone was screaming and running as chairs were being turned over. Someone had the presence of mind to call 911. Kelly and Bee couldn't believe their eyes. Guests were running everywhere. They looked around to see what was happening! There was Girl, Sweetheart and Halfpint! The trio came up to the gazebo. Bee went over and Kelly was close behind.

Bee said, "Hi Girl." Halfpint came running to her and jumped in her lap as Bee was now sitting on the gazebo steps.

"You made it; you are alright. You didn't starve," Bee exclaimed.

Barry had taken care of crowd control and escorted everyone into the house for their safety. He knew the cougars were not dangerous but everyone else didn't. Bee had a little visit with them. They were honored guests and played an important part in her life as well as Kelly's. They were so glad to see Halfpint was well again. They heard sirens in the background and the family told Girl to go. She was not moving. Pa sternly spoke and told Girl she was in danger and she should go; now! The family tried to stay between the gazebo and the mansion so people could not see what was happening. You can imagine the photos that would have been taken. It would have looked too suspicious.

Girl listened to Pa as he had not lost his touch with her, and she disappeared down the hill and into the gorge.

Pastor Bill was still in the gazebo praying. He could not believe what was transpiring before his eyes. He would never experience another wedding like this one! The police arrived with guns drawn. Barry told them the danger was over as the cougars had left. He relayed the same message to the ambulance and the Firefighters.

Bee and Kelly were ecstatic to know their little Halfpint was well again and part of Girl's family. As they turned around and saw the mess that had been left by their guests, it became apparent that they would have some explaining to do. The first reaction to the overturned seating was shock, but they soon found the humor in it and laughed hysterically. The family couldn't help but join them in spontaneous laughter.

The laughter was suddenly disrupted by multiple loud shots. They were all terrified and knew the shots would be directed at the cougar family.

"Barry, can you find out who is shooting?" Shawn pleaded.

He went to make some calls and found it was a search party sent out to capture the cougar. Barry gave orders for the search to stop and for the search party to disband. How were they going to go on with the wedding? Barry suggested he and Mark go down and check it out. Barry and Mark borrowed and quickly put on some of Shawn's casual wear, and left through Pa's study entrance to the caves. Josh and some friends set up all the overturned chairs and picked up the musical in-struments. The musicians started to play and the festive mood began to return with great apprehension. Shawn made an announcement that there was no danger and they should all have a good time. It was up to Bee and Kelly to set the mood for the evening, and hide their angst regarding the cougars' safety. They would let everyone eat first and mingle to lessen the anxiety of the evening. Pa blessed the food and the newly married couple. He also mentioned they would have their kiss as it was interrupted during the ceremony. If anyone wanted photos, they could take them now. It kick-started the wedding atmo-sphere again and everyone loosened up. Kelly spoke with his family assuring them that everything was fine. They, as well as the others, had never experienced something like that before.

Bee and Kelly had their first dance after the meal. The atmo-sphere was one of guarded relaxation. Dad and Bee had their dance. Kelly's Mom didn't dance, so he and his Mom stood and chatted. It was a symbol of time spent together, honoring who they were to each other and all the memories that led to this moment.

The wedding party dance was on hold, as Mark had not returned yet. Angela asked where he was, and Dad told her he was sent to take care of something. Dad was thanking all the special guests like Kelly's family and those that had come from Italy, Germany, and South America.

He noticed Barry and Mark and announced the wedding party dance and that everyone should join in.

"What did you find?" Shawn asked Barry.

"The three are fine and held up in the first grassy ledge where Vinnie fell. It looked like Girl was grazed by a bullet and has a flesh wound. Have you ever thought that they are getting too tame and too familiar with your family? Their lives could be in danger if you continue to befriend them," Barry insisted.

Shawn was taken back and of course knew this was true. The family was too taken up with the tameness of these three. Pa's needs while hiding and the emergencies the cougars had, caused them to lose sight of the fact that the cougars needed to be elusive and stay hidden from humans. He assured Barry they would do a better job at keeping the cougars wild. Of course, Bee and Kelly couldn't wait to hear and were very relieved at the outcome. They could concentrate on their guests and the beginning of a new life together.

Josh and Carly led in the dance as well as Mac and Mark. Bee was so proud of her brother and the man he was becoming. She thought he and Mac sure made a nice couple, as they switched partners to dance with one another. She wondered if a spark of romance would ever be ignited between them in the future. Carly and Dustin were an item, and Mitchell seemed to be interested in a guest as well. Fritz and Hannah fit in with Josh, Mark and Mac, like a dirty shirt. Lauren was radiant with her long hair and aqua gown. She and Joel were noticeable from the rest with their South American dance moves. They were a pleasure to watch. Bee danced with her Dad and Pa and felt like life was never going to be the same again. She knew their love would always be there, but she also knew she and Kelly could now make their way in life. It turned out to be perfect even with the craziness of the cougars showing up. You could always tell that when guests were having a fabulous time and getting lost in the moment, it meant the evening was a success. At the end of the evening, everyone held hands high and made and arch for Bee and Kelly to walk through, wishing them well.

The guests left chatting and discussing all aspects of the wedding, the good and the bad. Kelly's family left that evening since he had not been able to persuade them to stay the night. They felt if they got back in time for the morning, they could relieve their neighbors. Jake made a special effort to get a small bus to transport the large family in comfort. Kelly was so grateful that they were in good hands as they said their goodbyes.

All of the guests from abroad left for the airport that evening, as they had packed earlier. There were heartfelt goodbyes. Everyone cried as their bonds had strengthened during the past week.

Bee and Kelly would stay in Niagara Falls for a couple of nights. In a few weeks they would fly out to Rio de Janeiro. Lauren and Joel had given them a wedding gift of staying at their guesthouse for a week. They were happy to see the marvels of this beautiful city and see what Josh and Pa and the others had done there.

Bee and Kelly the honeymooners, time away was awesome. They walked the beach and took the aerial car as well as seeing all the other sights in Rio. They were left to themselves on the second floor and enjoyed the private space. The views were out of this world and they pinched themselves many times that they were actually there. Lauren made them feel so at home and special.

Afterwards, they would stay at home in Bee's room until their exams were written. They would work hard to finish these courses and wanted to get that off of their list of things to do. It would be a grueling time studying for their exams, but they would be together. That is what mattered.

After the wedding, things had quieted down, and Kelly and Bee were back. Dad called a family meeting, including Grammy and Grammpy. They now knew all the secrets and would have to know this too. Dad mentioned that the family should distance themselves from the cougars, for the animal's safety. It was obvious that they were getting too familiar with humans. It was a chapter that they would have to close, as enjoyable as it was for both humans and cougars. Everyone was sad about this but totally understood after the wedding fiasco.

Dad mentioned how fortunate it was that no one got a picture of the tame cougars and of Halfpint sitting on Bee's lap, even if it was an adorable moment. Bee smiled recalling the moment and how it felt.

Dad continued, "The next item is about Mary, Mitchell and Dustin. They are well settled into this country. The boys are enjoying their work. As a matter of fact, Mary and Angela are getting along very well. The boys have decided, now that they have some money, that they will buy the Snider House in Queenston. It has a large barn. They want to convert the top floor into a loft apartment. Dustin and Carly have plans to marry in the near future, and it suits their needs. The house will have a mother-in-law suite, and Mitchell will renovate the rest of it to suit him and that special girl he was so keen on at the wedding. The boys can use the bottom of the barn for their vehicles, tools and a work shop.

We are going to be sorry to see Mark and Angela move.

"What?! No one told me!" Josh gasped.

"I know Josh, Angela just told me a couple of hours ago. Mark and Angela have given it much thought over the last weeks and Angela thought that they should buy a property to invest some of their money in. The city is selling the property next door on the other side of the ravine. They had put an offer in and were just told they got the property. Every other buyer seemed to be afraid of the cougars. Is that close enough for you, Josh?" Dad asked.

"Yes, it is, I am so relieved. But there is no house," Josh asked.

"That is the good part. They would like to have one built on the property," Dad replied.

Josh was excited and thought that he and Mark would have to investigate that property some more in the future.

"Now, to the next item on hand. We have not had time to ask in private, but your mother and I wondered if you wanted to live in the carriage house?" Dad asked, looking at Kelly. "As a matter of fact, you now have the money to buy it if you so desire."

Bee got ecstatic. They were going to rent a small apartment, but this would be so nice. It would have lots of room for Kelly's family to visit. She was delighted and wouldn't mind staying at Mom and Dad's until Mark's house was finished. They would dedicate their time to finishing school. By the time they could move into the carriage house, they would have a totally new start without having to study.

"Yes, we would love to buy the carriage house!" Bee exclaimed, looking at Kelly nodding his head.

Everyone was excited, and life couldn't get better.

Josh excused himself and texted Mac. She would be right over. Mark, Mac and Josh would need to check out the property they had just bought. We went down around the old gazebo and into the ravine to where the pump house stood on the edge of Mark's property, adjacent to ours. We hadn't been down there since the days we played hide and go seek. The door creaked open. It was deeper than we remembered. The rusty old relic of a pump was still in place sitting on wooden planks on the ground. There was lots of room in behind it, and we wondered why. We shone our flashlights to see if we could find anything odd. The whole back wall seemed to be a unit of its own. Josh pushed on it. It moved easily. One side pushed in but only two feet. We had to squeeze in through the narrow opening. The lights searched our new surroundings. It looked like another tunnel!

"This is on my property," Mark explained.

"I wish there were secrets on my property," pouted Mac.

"Someday we will check that out too," suggested Josh, looking around.

They decided to follow the tunnel that took a sudden turn towards the gorge and downward. Mark was beside himself with excitement.

"Mark, settle down," commanded Josh.

"Hey, this is an awesome surprise, don't you think?" he said.

"For sure!" Mac agreed, "where do you think we will end up?"

We kept on going until we were walking on level rock. We had lost our sense of direction and Josh didn't have his compass. Off of the tunnel there was a cave like room with rags in it. We examined them and wondered who they belonged to. There were sacks in the corner. We picked them up, but nothing lay under them. The tunnel continued until we were at the water level.

"We could fish from here," exclaimed Mark."

They noticed a small old wooden boat in the brush against the rock ledge. It had deteriorated over time. They peeked underneath and found an old canteen of water and knapsack made from an old sack. It looked like an animal had been into it years before and eaten whatever they found. There were a few coins on the ground beside the handmade knapsack. They looked like the coins we found in our tunnels! Mark picked up the coins examining them carefully and put them in his pocket.

"It looks like whoever wanted to use this didn't make it," said Josh.

"Maybe it was that soldier that had the bars of gold to give to the ancestors?" Mac questioned.

That could be, we thought. They did say he knew the way out if he used dynamite for the boulder.

"If there is one tunnel, do you think there are more?" asked Mark.

Josh and Mac thought that was a big possibility.

"Maybe they join to your tunnels!" Mark said with confidence.

"These are your tunnels, Mark, so what do you want us to say about them, if anything? asked Josh.

Mark decided that secrecy is important for safety, as he learned that firsthand. These tunnels could have belonged to a totally separate group of prisoners or to the same ones they had already found. He would, of course have to tell his mother after a while, as well as Pa and Josh's Dad. Pa didn't say he found information on the tunnel, only that the government was looking for money buried on the land. But this was many years ago. It was also dangerous if this story was revived. The three were delighted with their find and decided that they would put old pieces of wood and other things in front of the back wall of the pump house. It would make the entrance less obvious. Mark was also going to ask Dad and Pa about putting an access down from his house to the tunnel. They seemed pretty good at figuring all that out and doing it in secrecy. The three friends figured they would not be bored in the days to come. They were in a good place at a good time and surrounded by good people. Right now, it was all they needed.

Acknowledgments

I have a special place in my assortment of gratitude for Barry Wills, for taking the time to edit my last book! At a very busy time in his life, Barry did this for me as a personal favour. Thank you for using one of your many gifts and completing my book in this way. Your work is so much appreciated.

I could not see this book published without thanking my greatest supporter, my strength at all times: Harry, my one and only since we were teens, has been the one that has held me when I needed to be held and let me fly when that was what I wanted. I am forever grateful for such a strong man when I needed one. I am even more in awe of the tenderness that he shows at just the right times.

With all my love and appreciation,
Marg

About the Author

Margarete Ledwez was born in Germany, emigrating to Canada with her parents and brother when she was just a year old. She quickly developed a longing to create which has eventually manifested itself in her writing.

Growing up in St. Catharines, Ontario, she became fascinated by the tunnels that had been used to hide slaves as part of the Underground Railroad and later by bootleggers during Prohibition.

While she and her husband were raising their own children they lived in Niagara Falls, just 5 kilometers from the celebrated *Screaming Tunnel.* Her curiosity was once again piqued when she discovered the myths and legends surrounding the many tunnels under the famous falls, and when writing this series of stories, she drew from her knowledge as well as her unending intrigue that there could be many more tunnels yet to be discovered.

Death and Redemption is Margarete Ledwez's third novel, the final book in this series about the mysteries of the tunnels under Niagara Falls. The story has been evolving in the author's imagination for many years.

Margarete Ledwez lives in St. Catharines, Ontario with her husband, Harry.

Other Books by Margarete Ledwez

Past Secret Present Danger:
What Deadly Secrets Lie in the Tunnels Beneath
Niagara Falls?

Niagara Tunnels Secrets Revealed:
A Josh and Mac Mystery Adventure in Niagara Falls